T0149381

EMBERS ON THE HEARTH

WRITTEN BY
FRANCES BORICCHIO

ILLUSTRATED BY
ASHLEY NERSESIAN

AuthorHouse™
1663 Liberty Drive
Bloomington, IN 47403
www.authorhouse.com
Phone: 1 (800) 839-8640

Published by AuthorHouse 11/20/2018

ISBN: 978-1-5462-6981-6 (sc)
ISBN: 978-1-5462-6980-9 (e)

Library of Congress Control Number: 2018913932

Print information available on the last page.

This book is printed on acid-free paper.

ACKNOWLEDGMENTS

I would like to thank my great-niece, Ashley Nersesian, for her artwork on this project. Her thoughtful time spent on the creation of each illustration helps make the story come alive.

I would also like to thank my niece Jolene Nersesian for her encouragement and input in the story.

And I thank my husband Barry Boricchio for his encouragement, story input, and help with critiquing the storytelling and dialogue. He is also the illustrator of the final picture at the end of the story.

This book is dedicated to my sister Rosalie Fauss. She wanted to be a writer of western novels, but tragically, she passed away before seeing her dream realized. She had an idea for a story that was to be titled "Embers on the Hearth," which would follow the life and times of a trapper named Jason McIvers.

It was always in the back of my mind to someday write Rosalie's story for her, and one day I began. A bittersweet part of this undertaking is that Rosalie's nineteen-year-old granddaughter Ashley Nersesian, who was born after Rosalie passed away, is the illustrator of this book. Rosalie's daughter, Jolene Nersesian, contributed to the storyline.

I will never know where Rosalie's story would have taken the reader, but I think this is one possibility.

CHAPTER 1

Jason McIvers woke to the familiar surroundings in the guardhouse. He rubbed his hand across his bearded chin and wondered how long it had been this time. He focused his eyes on the water bucket to his left and dipped the cup into it, stopping to remove a bug from the cup before drinking. He stared at the cup and threw it across the cell. The water did not take care of the gnawing hunger in his stomach.

He noticed he was alone in the cell. Usually, there was at least one other man there. Jason tried to remember how he had come to be in this all-too-familiar cell. He smiled as he figured he had drunk himself into a fight, which usually ended with him tossed into the guardhouse to sleep it off.

Jason stood up and tested his legs. They were a little weak, but he'd be all right. He would pay his fine and sit through another one of the colonel's lectures about his savage and barbaric ways, and then he would go back to the hills and tend his traps. In time, he would have enough furs to bring back to the fort to sell. With the money he got for the furs, he'd go to Ike's Saloon to drink away the long days spent in the hills and maybe engage in a fight or two. It was always the same; it was the only life he knew.

Jason heard the door to the outer cell open and saw the guard approach. He was a young boy who had probably just come out from the east for his first assignment at a fort. The young boy cleared his throat, faced Jason, and said, "Colonel wants to see you."

"Doesn't he always?" Jason asked. He picked up his hat and ran his fingers through his hair. "Come on, boy, open this door," he said. "I've seen this place long enough."

The guard said nothing as he opened the door and let Jason out. In the front office, Jason spied his rifle. He went to reach for it, but the guard stopped him and said, "I'm sorry, sir, but I'm to take you straight to the colonel."

Jason flashed the guard a curious look. Defiantly, he walked over and picked up his rifle and then went out the door. The fort hadn't changed any. It was still the same hot, dusty place. He looked around the compound. It was small in comparison to some of the other forts, but it was neat and well kept. There were a few buildings to house the soldiers, a mess hall, the telegraph office, a general store, Ike's Saloon, the stable, Miss Ellie's place for fine eating, the trading post where Jason sold his furs, the bathhouse, and of course, the guardhouse.

The fort was surrounded by a huge wooden fence. A few soldiers stood on a catwalk at the top of the fence with their rifles pointed toward the barren plain. To the right was a large lookout tower with one soldier standing inside, his eyes fixed on the desolate land. Suddenly, the guard in the tower stiffened and shaded his eyes against the sun to make out more clearly what he had seen. Soon the soldier yelled down to the others at the gate, "Riders comin'! Open the gate."

A dozen soldiers on horseback rode past Jason. He watched them pass with their sabers clanking inside their scabbards. They had entered the only civilization around for miles. Jason watched the soldiers dismount, and the lieutenant hurried into the colonel's office. Jason was aware of the guard behind him.

"Mr. McIvers, can we go now?" asked the guard. "The colonel is waiting."

Jason put his arm around the young solider and laughed. "All right, boy, let's go. I'm kind of curious as to what that lieutenant is in such a hurry for."

As they approached the colonel's office, Jason saw the sign above the door: "Colonel Tyson Ashby— Commander, Fort Ryerson." When they entered the office, another officer looked at him and told him to be seated. Jason eyed the mirror on the wall and walked over to it. He looked closely, as if for the first time, at himself. Tired brown eyes stared back at him. He rubbed his cheek with the palm of his hand and groaned. He never had liked beards; they only look good on colonels. He grinned and flashed a row of straight white teeth as he smiled to himself. His brown hair was sun-bleached to a honey color, but it was dirty and matted from his visit to the guardhouse. He'd get cleaned up after he talked to the colonel.

The door opened, and the officer motioned for Jason to come in. "The colonel will see you now."

Jason strode past the soldier and entered the colonel's office. The colonel was seated at an oversized oak desk, and behind him hung the flag of the States. The colonel was a stout man with a white beard. He was dressed smartly in a blue uniform with polished brass buttons down the front of his jacket. Jason could see just a hint of the large yellow sash around his rounded belly.

Colonel Ashby stood up and pointed to a chair by the desk. "Sit down, Mr. McIvers," he ordered.

Jason sat and eyed the lieutenant at the window. He too was smartly dressed, except for the dust that covered his uniform from the day's ride.

"McIvers," the colonel said.

Jason held up a hand to the colonel and said, "I know. Just tell me how bad I busted up Ike's place, and I'll pay for the damages."

The colonel sat back down and leaned back in his chair. He took a deep breath before he said, "It's not that simple this time, McIvers."

Jason looked at the colonel and studied him for a while. His face was set with tight lips, and he had a serious look about him. "What do you mean, 'not that simple'?" Jason asked.

The lieutenant at the window turned to face Jason and said, "Damn it, McIvers. Don't play innocent with us. Don't think you can excuse yourself from murder."

Jason's eyes narrowed as he looked at the lieutenant and asked, "What do you mean by *murder*?"

The lieutenant roared, "I mean Ike Davis! You rode in and shot up his place and killed Ike!"

Jason stood up, and his chair overturned as he slammed his fist down on the desk and said, "Look, soldier boy, I don't hold kindly to a man who says I killed someone, and I don't hold kindly to a man like you all decked out in your finery, riding around on that fine horse of yours, thinking there ain't no one fit to wipe your boots."

The Lieutenant's voice lowered to a growl. "And what about you?" he said to Jason. "You come from the hills with your furs, and you turn this compound into your own personal playground. You think because you're up in those hills all the time that it earns you the right to come down here and do what you please?"

Jason grabbed the lieutenant by the collar and pulled him close. The nerve in his cheek twitched.

Colonel Ashby quickly stood up and broke the two apart. "Sit down, McIvers. Lieutenant, go outside and cool off. I wish to speak to Jason alone."

The lieutenant straightened his collar and grabbed his hat as he walked out the door, slamming it behind him.

The colonel looked at Jason and said, "McIvers, I won't tolerate such outbursts in my office."

"Tell that jackass lieutenant of yours to back off and quit making accusations he can't back up," Jason said angrily. "Now I know I was in Ike's place, and I know I broke the place up in that fight, but I didn't kill anyone."

The colonel looked at him and said, "Not directly, no."

"What do you mean, 'not directly'?" Jason's voice was rising now. "Damn it, Colonel, stop playing this cat-and-mouse game with me. Tell me straight out, what happened to Ike?"

The colonel's voice was low as he spoke. "Ike was killed during the fight. He must have caught a stray bullet when the shootin' started."

"Get to the point, Colonel," Jason pushed.

"The point is, McIvers, every time you come into this fort, you get drunk at Ike's place and make a shambles of it." The colonel hesitated. "If you weren't here to start all that ruckus, Ike would be alive today."

Jason eyed the colonel and said, "You're saying I didn't kill Ike, but it's my fault he's dead?"

"Well," the colonel said.

"Damn it!" Jason roared.

"Yes!" the colonel shouted. "Yes! That's what I'm saying!" The colonel lowered his voice. "I think it would be better if you weren't seen at the fort anymore. I think it would be best if you cleared out."

"Cleared out?" Jason said. "You know there isn't another outpost within a hundred miles of here. Where do I sell my furs? Or have you forgotten that's how I make a living?"

The colonel took a deep breath and let it out slowly before answering. "No, I didn't forget." He turned to face the window, his hands clasped behind him. "McIvers, I'm going to make you a proposition. I've got something very important that has to get to Fort Cross. You can take it there for me, and I'll pay you, of course."

Jason stared at the colonel and asked, "And what if I say no?"

"Then you answer for Ike's death," the colonel said.

Suddenly, the situation was clear to Jason. The colonel needed him to ride to Fort Cross, and these trumped-up charges were just to make sure that he took the job. "Colonel," Jason said, "why me? Why don't you send that pompous lieutenant? I'm sure he'd jump at the chance."

"He doesn't know the hills as good as you do," the colonel replied.

"The hills? What's wrong with going across the flatlands?" Jason asked.

The colonel turned to face Jason. "Lieutenant Straton and his men just came back from patrol; he says there are Indian signs all over the prairie. So if you take the hills along with a man of mine, you'll get through. A small party of men crossing over the flatlands would surely be seen. They'd be cut down before they got halfway to Fort Cross."

Jason thought about this. He couldn't figure what would have brought the Indians out of the hills. He had trapped there for years, and he'd never been bothered. True, he'd seen signs now and then, but he'd never come across Indians. He looked at the colonel and said, "We have a treaty with them, and we've had no trouble since it was signed. If the treaty was broke, they didn't break it. They'd have more to lose than us." Jason thought about the signs the lieutenant had seen. "What signs did the lieutenant see out there, Colonel?"

Colonel Ashby stared at his desk. "Straton found the payroll detail a ways out. They were all killed, and the payroll was gone."

Jason cocked his head. "Wait a minute. What makes

you think it was Indians that did it? I never knew an Indian who'd kill for money. Money means nothing to them."

"The money was in the saddlebags, and the saddlebags were gone," the colonel said. "They probably didn't even know what was in them. Besides, they were all killed with arrows."

Jason said quietly, as if to himself, "Don't make no sense, them comin' out of the hills like that."

The colonel looked at Jason and said, "Regardless of how much sense it makes, McIvers, it's been done, and I need your answer now. Will you take the job?"

Jason sighed and said, "Well, I sure don't want to answer for a murder I didn't commit. And I don't like the way you've backed me into a corner like this. But I'll do it."

The colonel let out a sigh of relief and said, "Good, good."

With that the colonel turned to the large safe standing in the corner of the office. He spun the dial around a few times, then lifted the long handle up and outward. He brought out a valise and carried it to the desk.

Jason moved closer to see what was in it. The colonel looked at Jason. His hands seemed to be caressing the valise. "This is my daughter's dowry," he said. "She is to be married at Fort Cross in one week. I was going to send it with a small party of men until Lieutenant Straton gave me his report on the payroll detail. That's why I decided that you and Lieutenant Straton would have the best chance of getting through."

Jason's eyes widened. "Wait a minute, Colonel. Not

Straton. There is something about that man that does not set well with me."

The colonel quickly answered, "I need a man with military authority to go along."

"All right," Jason said, "but not that quick-headed fool. Give me Sergeant Emory or Lieutenant Swane. I won't have that man along to slow me down!"

The colonel looked at him and said, "Regardless of how you feel about him, he's going." The colonel hesitated, as if not wanting to say any more. He raised his eyes to meet Jason's as he continued. "I cannot leave the post at this time. And that means that I cannot give my daughter away at the ceremony. Lieutenant Straton is a friend of the family, and he has offered to stand in my place. My daughter has agreed. She is not very happy about me not being able to attend her wedding. Frankly, I'm not very happy about it either, but Washington isn't as compassionate about such matters as I am."

Jason smiled and said, "You're just full of surprises, aren't you, Colonel?"

"No matter what you may think, it's important that both the money and the lieutenant reach Fort Cross safely," the colonel replied.

"Does Straton know about this new route you want me to take?" Jason asked.

"He knows," the colonel replied, "and if it will make you feel any better, McIvers, he is just as unhappy about it as you are. But with things the way they are, it's the only way. He doesn't know those hills as well as you do, and as I said, it is most important that you reach there safely."

Jason gave him a reassuring look. "When do we leave, Colonel? Tomorrow?"

"Yes," said the colonel. "Oh, and McIvers, I'd like to wish you luck."

Jason sneered, "With Straton along, I'll need more than luck."

Jason excused himself from the colonel's office. While walking across the compound, he saw Lieutenant Straton leaning against a wall. Straton's hair was black, and he had a black mustache that seemed to split his face in two. His chin was free of any beard, and the deep cleft in it was clearly visible. His shoulders were not as broad as Jason's, but he was just as tall.

Their eyes met, and a cold feeling came over Jason. *Arrogant fool*, Jason thought as he stared at him. Jason knew they would tangle someday.

Jason headed for the bathhouse.

CHAPTER 2

In the morning Jason made his way to the colonel's office. He entered to find Lieutenant Straton already there. The two men eyed each other. Straton smiled, but Jason did not return the greeting.

"I didn't recognize you, McIvers, with all that dirt off. And what happened to your beard? It's too bad you can't figure out how to stay clean all the time."

Jason glared at him and said, "My way of life is not the cleanest, but it's honest work. It's a pity you don't know anything about that."

Straton stiffened as he clenched his fist.

Colonel Ashby said, "Cool off, Lieutenant. You deserved that. I suggest the two of you make peace between yourselves. The both of you will be depending on each other to reach Fort Cross in safety." Colonel Ashby looked at Lieutenant Straton. "I should think you would put aside all your feelings toward this man to ensure your safe arrival at Fort Cross."

"Colonel Ashby," the lieutenant said, "I don't need

him to lead me into the hills. Besides, what's to stop him from taking the money himself after we are well into the hills and away from civilization?"

Jason banged his fist on the table. "Damn it, Colonel! I didn't ask for this job, and I didn't ask for Straton to accompany me. If you want your daughter's dowry to reach Fort Cross, I'll take it, and if I have to take this arrogant jackass with me, that's fine too. But I don't need his cheap talk." Jason checked the anger in his voice as he said to the colonel. "Now get that valise out here, and let's get going."

Colonel Ashby took the valise out of the safe and placed it on the desk.

Jason opened the case and put the money in his saddlebags. Once they were filled, he slung them over his shoulder and extended his hand to the colonel. "It's best we start now, Colonel. I have my horse outside." He turned to Straton. "You ready?"

Straton nodded his head. He too extended a hand to the colonel and then turned to leave. When he reached the door, the colonel stopped him.

Jason heard the colonel say to Straton, "Lewis, give my love to Martha and tell her how sorry I am that I can't be there on the day of her wedding."

Straton smiled and said, "I will, sir." He walked outside, where Jason was securing the saddlebags on his horse.

Jason mounted his horse and said to Lieutenant Straton, "All this time, I never knew you had a first name."

Straton gave him an angry stare, got on his horse, and said to Jason, "There's a lot of things you don't know about me, McIvers." He spurred his horse and rode off toward the gate.

Jason shook his head and rode after him as he heard the familiar call from the guard tower: "Open the gate!" The two men rode out as the gate closed quickly behind them.

It was sundown when the two men made camp. Lieutenant Straton gathered some small sticks to make a fire. He was ready to light the wood when Jason stopped him.

"No fires, Straton."

"How are we gonna eat?" Straton asked.

Jason went to his saddlebags and pulled out some jerky. He tossed Straton a piece. "We eat this," Jason said. "Too risky for a fire. Indians can spot it a mile away."

Straton looked at him. "The Indians are out of the hills. We got no problem. Besides, I can't eat this stuff; it's like leather."

Jason stared at him. "Better get used to it 'cause there'll be no fires."

Jason removed the saddle from his horse and took the saddle, his bedroll, and the saddlebags to a spot under a tree. He placed the blankets on the ground and put the saddlebags under his saddle, which he would use for a pillow. He stretched out on the blankets and slid his hat over his eyes.

"You take the first watch," Jason said to Straton. "Wake me in a couple of hours."

Jason had been asleep for about an hour when the smell of smoke woke him up. His eyes flew open, and he saw Straton in front of a small fire, rubbing his hands together close to the flames. Jason rose and ran toward the fire. He kicked the sticks apart and stomped out the fire with his boot.

"You fool!" he yelled at Straton. "That fire can be seen for miles! You want our scalps on the lance of some buck? Get your things together. We're leaving."

Straton looked at Jason and said, "I haven't had any sleep."

"You should have thought of that before you lit that fire," Jason said.

Jason was saddling his horse when he heard a branch on the ground crackle, followed by a faint sound of leaves rustling. He froze. Jason turned his eyes to Straton. By the look on the lieutenant's face, Jason knew he'd heard it too.

"Indians?" Straton whispered to Jason.

Jason shook his head. "If it were Indians, we'd be dead by now."

Jason eased his gun from his holster and cocked it. Straton did the same.

A voice called from the trees beyond their camp. "Drop your guns and kick them away from you, and put your hands up."

Straton dropped his gun and kicked it away. Jason gave him an angry stare and did the same. Four men advanced toward them, two with rifles and two with pistols. Jason eyed the four men. Three of them, he didn't recognize, but the one who did the talking was familiar to him.

The familiar man said, "If you don't want to get hurt, do as we say and hand over those saddlebags. All we want is the money." Just then, Jason remembered where he had seen this man before. It had been in Ike's Saloon. He was a drifter by the name of Travis.

"We have no money here, but if you want the saddlebags you can have them," Jason replied. He walked over to Straton's bedroll and reached for the lieutenant's saddlebags.

Travis's gun went off, and a bullet hit the ground at Jason's right boot heel. "Not those," he said. He pointed his gun toward Jason's bedroll. "Yours."

Jason walked to his bedroll, lifted his saddle, and picked up the saddlebags. He thought, *How? How did he know?*

"Cover him," Travis said.

Jason handed him the saddlebags.

Travis's eyes lit up as he opened the saddlebags and saw the money. A smile came across his lips. "It's here. It's all here, just like you said, Lew."

Jason's eyes widened as he turned to Straton.

"Shut up, you fool," Straton barked at Travis as he cast a nervous glance toward Jason. "I don't know what he's talking about."

Travis looked at Straton. "Drop the bull, Lew. He'd have figured it out anyway. I brought the clothes like you told me. So get out of them army duds and put these on."

Straton walked toward Travis. "He wasn't supposed to know I was in on it, Travis. This was supposed to look like a holdup."

Jason stared at Straton. "Did you plan that massacre with the payroll detail too? Made it mighty easy for you to be the one who found them and reported to the colonel it was Indians. You planned that, same as you planned this. What else have you got planned?"

"No one will ever think different about the payroll detail than what I said," Straton answered.

"Yeah," Travis said, "we filled those soldier boys with so many arrows, we got the whole fort thinking it was them Injuns who done it." Travis walked to his horse and took a bow and arrow from his saddlebag. He turned toward Jason and said, "And when they find you with an arrow stuck in your belly, they'll think them Injuns are really on the warpath."

Straton looked at Travis and said, "You're not going to kill him, are you?"

"Well, what do you think we should do?" Travis answered. "He knows too much. What if he gets to Colonel Ashby and tells him that you were the one who hit that payroll detail? And what will he do when he finds out you took off with his daughter's dowry? You think on that before you say we shouldn't kill him."

Straton was silent for a moment. "Tie him up for now," he said. "We'll decide what to do with him later."

When Jason was secured, Straton, Travis, and the other three men began counting the money.

"What took you so long with that fire, Lew?" Travis asked.

Straton jerked a thumb at Jason. "He was afraid it would attract Indians."

Travis laughed. "Yeah, well, we almost lost you back there in the dark."

"You got the horses and supplies?" Straton asked.

"I got 'em holed up at that place where we hid the

payroll," Travis said. "The sooner we get going, the closer we are to Mexico. And the sooner we get rid of him, the safer we'll be." Travis pointed to Jason.

"Couldn't we just take his horse and water and let him go?" Straton asked.

"He's only a day from the fort," Travis said. "He could make that easy. Damn it, Lew, don't go soft on us now. We've got too much at stake to let him spoil it. Now get over there and untie him."

Straton walked toward Jason and knelt down behind him, working to free the ropes. "This wasn't supposed to happen, McIvers. I'm sorry," he said.

"You can stop it if you want," Jason said. "Just give me a gun and move away. I'll run toward the trees, and you can say I got away from you and took your gun."

"Won't work," Travis said, appearing beside Straton. Jason could see the bow in his hand. "Stand up," Travis said.

Jason stood as his mind raced. Straton was still standing behind him.

"Get back, Lew," Travis said.

"Travis, wait. I—"

Straton's words were broken off when Jason threw a fist into his ribs. As Straton fell, Jason grabbed for the lieutenants gun.

Startled, Travis threw down the bow and reached for his gun. He drew and cocked it almost instantly, but Jason was already running for the trees. Jason heard Travis barking orders at the others. "Don't let him get away!"

Jason ran blindly into the trees and found himself approaching a cliff. He knew Straton's men were behind him. Jason edged toward the cliff and saw the river below. He had one chance. He had to jump into the river. He eyed a spot about ten feet away from him where the cliff cut in. It was the only place Jason could jump and clear the rocks. He was turning to run when he saw one of Straton's men. Jason cocked the gun and fired. The man grabbed at his chest as he fell to the ground.

"Over here! He's over here," a voice yelled from the darkness.

Jason pulled the trigger, but the gun didn't go off. He squeezed the trigger again but heard the click of an empty chamber.

"He's out of bullets!" someone shouted. "Rush him! Rush him!"

Jason threw the pistol at a man running toward him. As he ran for the edge of the cliff, a shot rang out. A fiery pain gripped Jason's side. He jumped down the gorge into the river. As soon as he hit the water, he began kicking his legs to bring himself to the surface. When his eyes were above the water, he looked for the shore and headed toward it, the pain still burning at his side. When he reached the shore, he pulled himself from the water. He was weak, and he shook his head, trying to clear his hazy eyes. The pain seized him once again. Jason's hand went to his side; he was bleeding.

Jason had to hide before Straton's men came looking for him. He crawled toward the rocks, but the pain took strength from him. He fought to stay conscious long enough to reach a safe place, but the pain was overpowering. He felt the darkness close in on him as he sank into unconsciousness.

CHAPTER 3

Jason woke with the sun in his eyes. There was a burning pain in his side. He felt a bandage when his hand moved to his side. He looked around slowly. He could hear the river, but he couldn't see it. He saw a tiny fire to his right and saw his own shirt on a rock. It had been washed. He propped himself up on one elbow and tried to piece together what had happened. He remembered Straton and the money, and he remembered jumping into the river, but after that his mind was a blank.

Someone has to be here, he thought as he rubbed his bandaged side.

Then he saw a rustling in the bushes in front of him. He looked for his gun but found only a rock. So he grabbed it to use as a weapon if need be. He waited in anticipation, his knuckles white around the rock. Then a figure emerged from the trees, and his hand went limp against the rock. Jason eyed the figure for a second and thought he saw a woman as he slowly lay back and shut his eyes. He lay still as he heard the footsteps come closer. He felt a hand against his forehead. Jason opened his eyes and was surprised to see that it was a woman, a young Indian woman. A smile came to Jason's lips. She was not fearful, but she kept her distance.

Slowly, she turned and went to the fire. She picked up a wooden bowl and began filling it from a small pot. She then walked back to Jason and knelt beside him, handing him the bowl. Jason tasted the food; it was good. He stared as she ate her food. She was a small lady with large brown eyes and long dark hair as black as a raven's wing. She wore a dress and moccasins made of buckskin. He couldn't help but notice how beautiful she was. Jason finished the food and set the bowl down beside him. He waited for her to speak, but she said nothing. Instead she got up and walked toward the river. She stopped to pick up a stick with a pointed end.

Jason knew she was going to catch some fish; he fished that way himself when he was in the hills. He would stand in the water, and when a fish came, he would spear it. Jason tried to stand. He wanted to go with her, but his legs were weak, and they buckled beneath him. Instantly, she dropped the stick and ran to him. She helped him lie back and pushed her hand against his chest as if to tell him to stay. When she knew he wouldn't move, she again picked up the stick. She turned toward Jason and allowed a smile to come to her lips, and then she ran toward the river.

Jason leaned back and smiled. He wondered who she was and where she had come from. He closed his eyes and pictured how pretty she was. With her face still fresh in his mind, he slowly drifted toward a peaceful sleep.

The days of Jason's healing passed quickly. He grew stronger each day. During that time Jason tried to speak to the Indian woman, but she never spoke a word to him. He tried speaking in the tongue of the few Indian tribes he knew, but either she was not of those tribes, or she couldn't speak.

Jason got used to her silence. He learned to read her eyes. They were gentle and calm, and they gave away her every emotion. She approached him to apply mud to his wound. She smiled when she saw how well the wound had healed. Jason watched as her smile began to fade, almost as if something bothered her. With the new dressing finished, she rose and walked to the fire. She retrieved the fish she had been cooking, placed some in a bowl, and handed it to Jason. Jason took the first piece and put it in his mouth. As always, she would not eat until he started. Jason smiled and nodded in approval; she could tell he liked the fish and returned his smile. Jason could see in her eyes that something was still bothering her.

With the meal completed, the Indian woman rose and walked to where she kept her things. Jason watched as she gathered her belongings and put them in a sack made of skins. She turned to Jason as he rose to his feet. He didn't understand what she was doing. She put her hand on her chest and pointed in the direction of the hills. Jason knew she was leaving. He had recovered enough, and there was nothing more she could do for him, but he didn't want her to go. He had never been so affected by anyone before or seen anyone as pretty as her. Jason remembered the sad look in her eyes when she'd noticed his wound was healing, and he wondered if she felt sad about leaving too.

Without thinking, Jason placed his hand on her shoulder. She didn't move. Jason was glad she was not afraid of him. Slowly, he reached for the sack she held, aware of her eyes fixed on him as he took the sack from her hand. He slowly, gently set it down. He hoped that this act would tell her he wanted her to stay. Still, she didn't move. Jason looked at her. *She is so special. She saved my life*, he thought.

"I know you don't understand," Jason said. "I can't explain what I feel, but I know I don't want you to go. Maybe I'm grateful for what you did for me; heck, maybe I'm just tired of being alone." Jason smiled. "You don't even know what I'm saying, do you? Well, maybe it's better that way, but I hope you can understand that I want you to stay."

As Jason stared at her, her eyes met his, and she smiled. Jason was happy; he knew she was not going to leave.

He looked at her and said, "I wish I knew your name. I wish I knew how you came to be here when I needed help. There is so much I'd like to know about you." Jason continued smiling at her. "Well, the first thing I'd like you to know about me is my name. It's Jason McIvers." He took her hand in his. "But you don't understand me, do you?"

"I understand you, Jason McIvers," she said.

Jason was surprised—almost startled—when she

spoke. Now it was Jason who was speechless. He pointed an accusing finger at her and said, "You can talk. All this time you never said a word. Why?"

Her head was bowed, and her eyes were fixed on the fringe hanging from her dress. She picked at it nervously. Colorful beads were perfectly sewn around the neckline on her dress. They outlined the beauty of her neck.

"The time of my mourning is over," she said. "The Gods had forbidden me to speak until the moon was whole again."

Jason thought of the full moon the night before. "Your husband died?" Jason asked.

She shook her head. "No I am not married. I mourn my father, chief of our people. It is a custom of our people to keep a silent mourning and never speak the name of the dead, so that the gods can guide his spirit to them." She raised her eyes and saw the look of confusion on Jason's face.

"The ways of my people are different from yours. For someone to speak the name of the dead before his soul can reach the spirits is a terrible thing, and the gods will not accept him and allow him to ride with the Great Ones for all eternity. If they hear his name before his spirit is received, all is lost. That is why we keep a silent mourning for our dead."

Jason stared at her. "Have you no family to be with during your mourning?" Jason asked.

"I am outcast from my people," she said. "I have shamed my family and denied my father a place with the Great Ones. While I was sleeping, my father's image came to me, and I spoke his name. My mother heard me,

FRANCES BORICCHIO

and soon all knew of my deed. I was sent away from my people. So I chose to walk the road to the Cave of the Great Ones, for if I can speak to them, maybe I can give my father his rightful place among the Great Ones, and then I can return to my people."

Jason said before thinking, "If you were asleep, how do you know you spoke his name?"

"You would doubt the wife of the chief?" she said with fire in her eyes. "My mother was strong in her grief. I was not, so I bear the burden of my loose tongue. I will never question the words of my mother."

Jason was sorry he had asked the question, but his curiosity had gotten the best of him. "You kept your silence all this time. Doesn't that matter?"

Some of the anger left her eyes as she replied, "It does not. I must go to the Cave of the Great Ones."

"Where is this cave?" Jason asked.

She pointed to the distant hills. Jason stared at them. He guessed there could be caves in those hills, but the distance astounded him. "That's a three-day ride from here," he said. "How do you plan to get there on foot?"

"I can carry water from the river, and I have food," she said.

Jason stared at her with disbelief. "You'll never make it alone."

"I will make it. I have to," she said as her brown eyes flashed at him.

Jason shook his head and said, "You're planning to cross miles of the worst godforsaken land anywhere in these parts. It's a rough trail for a man outfitted for the trip, but it'll be harder for us."

Her eyes met his in surprise. "You speak of us. You did not say before that you were going to the Cave of the Great Ones."

Jason felt uneasy about committing himself before thinking. He had his traps to tend to, and he should return to the fort to inform Colonel Ashby about what had happened. But this Indian woman made him feel something he had never felt before. The feeling was new to him, and he was a little afraid of it.

He shrugged off her comment and answered, "We'll have to do a little hunting along the way, maybe a rabbit or two. That sack you have is what we can carry water in. It's gonna be hard, though, with no gun for hunting."

"We have this," she said. Her hand slipped to the leather belt around her waist, and she pulled a knife from it.

Jason took the knife from her hand. He thought a while, then glanced at her bag of belongings. His eyes lit up as an idea came to him.

She stared at him, not knowing what he was thinking. He took the sack from her and put some sticks in it. She watched him work on his project. When he stepped back to admire it, she didn't know what it was.

"Well," he said, "what do you think?"

She stared at the contraption he had made. The top of the bag was held open by two sticks. Around the bottom of the sack, he had tied a small piece of twine. She still didn't understand.

Jason took a pebble and placed it inside the sack. "Look, pretend this pebble is a piece of meat. I put it in the sack. Something comes along and sees it. As it walks in to get the meat, I pull this twine, and the bag closes. Then all I do is step up to the bag and ..." He hit the bag to show her that anything inside would not come out alive. He looked up at her, and she smiled.

"Well, will it work with fish? We have no meat for bait," she joked. When she saw he wasn't amused, her smile left her face. "I did not mean to make fun of your trap. I am sorry."

"No need to be," he said. "Get some fish, and we'll test it."

They spent the next day in preparation for the trip. Jason built a travois, and together they tied food, water, and their belongings to it.

Soon they were on their way. Jason pulled the travois behind him. At midday, they stopped to rest. After they had rested a while, she rose and took the travois and began to pull it behind her.

"You're not going to pull that," Jason said. He attempted to take it from her, but she stopped him.

"I will take it from midday on, and you can take it in the morning," she said with determination. "It will be this way."

Jason knew she would not change her mind.

When there was an hour of daylight left, Jason said they should stop for the day. As Jason made a fire, she unloaded from the travois what they would need for the night. He watched her take the skin she used to lie on and the blanket she used for Jason's bedroll off the travois. She was undecided as to where to put them. She glanced at Jason, at the blanket, and then at a tree away from her. She stood there a moment before she unrolled her skin and laid it near the fire. Then she walked over to the tree and unrolled the blanket for Jason's bed.

She then went to the fish and began to prepare it. She felt Jason watching her, but when she turned to look at him, he looked away and stared into the fire.

Jason felt he should say something, and then it dawned on him that in all the time they had been together, she had never told him her name. He picked up a stick and poked at the fire. "Seems to me I told you my name a while back, but you never told me yours," he said.

"You never asked me," she said.

Jason drew his eyes from the fire and stared at her. He noticed she had moved closer to him and held a pot in her hand with the fish in it.

"Tikah," she answered.

Jason got up and took the pot from her, placing it on the fire as he let her name settle in his mind. *It's a pretty name*, he thought. *It fits her well.*

Jason watched Tikah as she turned the fish in the pot, her slender body bent forward. Her hair, unbraided now, spilled over her shoulders and fell down her arms. As he watched her, a feeling of protectiveness came over him.

"We've come a long way today," Jason said as he glanced at the sky. He noticed the clouds, red with color as dusk fell upon them. He remembered sitting alone under the same sky many times before when he was in the hills with his traps, but he had never noticed how pretty it was until now.

"It's going to be hot again tomorrow," Jason said. "Funny thing about these parts—it gets so dang hot during the day, but at night it's colder than a river of melted snow."

Tikah nodded in agreement as she handed him his bowl. Jason got a whiff of the food as he began to eat.

When the meal was finished, Jason stood and stretched. He again looked at the sky and noticed that the moon would soon replace the sun.

In a short while a million stars glittered above. *Sure is pretty*, he thought. "Well, I'm going to turn in and get some shut-eye," Jason said. "We've got a long walk ahead of us tomorrow." As he lay down, he noticed Tikah was still standing. "You should turn in too; we'll need a good night's rest for tomorrow."

"I would like to walk a little," she said.

"Do you want me to go with you?" Jason said, rising.

"No," Tikah said, holding up her hand. "I won't go far."

"Well, stay close," Jason said as he settled down into the warmth of the blanket.

It seemed like a long while before Tikah returned. Jason couldn't sleep while she was gone. Jason was beginning to develop feelings for Tikah. He wanted her near him. Tikah glanced at him for a moment she wanted to lay beside him but instead, she lay down on her skin near the fire. Jason was relieved she was back. He closed his eyes and fell asleep.

When he awoke, Jason shaded his eyes against the morning sun. He glanced from beneath the tree but did not see Tikah. His eyes searched around until he saw her. She had her back to him. She was by the fire, stirring breakfast in the pot.

"Good morning," Jason said.

"Good morning," she answered.

Jason got up and walked toward her. She spooned chunks of meat into a bowl and handed it to him. She said, "Your trap works well."

Jason smiled and started to eat, but he noticed she hadn't taken any food for herself. "Aren't you going to eat?" Jason asked.

"I have eaten already. I have a surprise for you," she said.

"A surprise? What is it?" Jason asked.

Tikah smiled and said, "Wait here." She walked over to where she slept and picked up a pouch. She returned to the fire and handed it to Jason.

He took the pouch and looked from it to her. "What is it?" he asked.

"Open it," she said.

Jason opened the pouch and found a small number of red berries in it.

"I found them this morning," Tikah said. "I picked as many as I could carry. They are very good. Taste one."

Jason took a few berries from the pouch and put them in his mouth. They were sweet. He handed the pouch to her, but she refused.

"No, they are for you. I ate some when I picked them off the bush," she said.

Jason put another in his mouth. He was happy she had found them. He looked at her smiling face and felt a little afraid. He told her, "You shouldn't go off like that alone. You don't know what's out there. It's not safe."

The smile left her face, and she said, "I thought you would be pleased."

Instantly, Jason knew he had hurt her feelings. He hadn't meant to, but he didn't want her to go off somewhere unless she said something to him first. He knew she could take care of herself, but that protective feeling still came over him again. *She's not like the women back at the fort. She don't need protectin'*, he thought. *Dadgum fool!*

Jason had been alone for so many years with no one to look out for but himself, no one to care for, especially a woman. Jason put the pouch down and said, "Tikah, I am very grateful for your surprise, and it's only that I wish no harm to come to you." He cupped her chin in his hand and said, "Thank you for the berries."

She quickly smiled at him and got up to reload the travois. Jason wasn't sure if he'd handled that right, but at least she had smiled at him again. He was happy about that.

The sun beat down hard on Jason's back as midday approached. He watched Tikah walking beside him. He couldn't believe her stamina. Any of the women from the fort would have tired out long before now, but she kept right up with him.

She spoke to him again of reaching the Cave of the Great Ones and how her people would rejoice when she told them she had set her father's spirit free to join the Great Ones. Jason stared off toward the mountains ahead. The cave seemed so far away, but Jason knew they could make it. When they stopped for a rest, Jason took the skin filled with water and drank slowly. The water felt cool against his dry lips. He handed the skin to Tikah, and she drank too.

Jason pointed and said, "Looks cooler over there."

Tikah nodded, and they walked toward a large rock. Tikah sat first and leaned her head against a huge stone. Jason was starting to sit beside her when he heard it, only for an instant—the vigorous beat of a rattle. His eyes followed the sound to where Tikah was sitting. A few inches away from her hand was a rattler, coiled and ready to strike. Jason grabbed her by the arm and violently pulled her away. She fell forward and watched as he quickly picked up a rock and smashed it against the snake's head. Jason stood for a while, ready to hit it again if need be, but the snake didn't move.

Jason turned toward Tikah. She was still on the ground and was rubbing her arm. He ran to her and grabbed her arm. "You didn't get bit, did you?" he asked.

"No," she said, "you pulled me away so fast, I fell on my arm. It's all right."

Relief filled Jason. He put his arms around Tikah and smiled. Jason was aware of her arms around him.

She looked at him and smiled. "We should be going," she said. "It is my turn to pull the travois."

"Not with your arm hurting like that." Jason started for the travois, but she stopped him.

"It does not hurt anymore." She reached for the rope, and they started once again.

They walked for some time without speaking a word. Jason thought about how terrible it would have been if she had been bitten by that snake. He shuddered and focused his eyes on the hills ahead.

CHAPTER **4**

The hills loomed big and gray against the sky as Jason and Tikah drew nearer to them. Slowly, they put the miles behind them. Each step moved them closer to the end of their journey. Jason stared ahead toward the hills. He guessed they were only a few hours away. He wondered what he would do after they reached the cave. Tikah would make her peace with the gods and then return to her people. He knew he would return to his trapping, but everything was so mixed up in his mind. He would have to make a decision soon, but either way, his life would be changed. If he returned to the hills and resumed his life the way it had been before, he would be lonely. He had grown used to the company of another. He thought of taking Tikah back with him, but that idea troubled him. His life was one where he never worried about anyone but himself, and with Tikah it would all be different.

Jason's eyes wandered to Tikah as she stood by the

fire, preparing supper. He smiled to himself and knew his mind was made up.

With the evening meal out of the way, Jason sat and rested his head against a tree. He stared at Tikah and thought of all the different ways he could tell her of his plan. He tested a few on himself, but the words were not coming out right, so Jason decided to let it go until another time. He noticed Tikah staring off into the distance.

"What are you looking at?" he asked her.

"I'm not sure," she said, "but look toward the hills. It looks like a light."

Jason stared out into the darkness, but he did not see a light. "I don't see anything," he answered.

"Look again. It comes and goes," she said while keeping her eyes fixed on a spot off in the distance.

But Jason still saw nothing.

Tikah stared for quite a while longer. "It is gone now. I don't see it anymore."

Jason looked at her and asked, "What kind of light did you see?"

"It was small," she answered. "Could there be someone out there?"

Jason answered, "Don't know, but whatever it is, we'll find out by afternoon tomorrow."

Tikah turned to him. "Tomorrow," she said, "when we get to the Cave of the Great Ones, I must go alone."

Jason stared at her with wide-open eyes of surprise and said, "I'm not letting you go into those hills alone."

"Please," she said, "I have to do this for myself and my family. I cannot allow you to come with me."

Jason got up from his bedroll and said, "And I cannot allow you to go up there alone." He turned to face her and put his hands on her shoulders, "Don't you know it could be dangerous?"

"Dangerous, yes," she said, "but I must go alone."

That determined look appeared in her eyes, but Jason ignored it. He had seen that stubborn look before when they argued about who was going to pull the travois. "Well, get some sleep now, and we will talk more about it in the morning," Jason said.

Tikah nodded in silent agreement.

Jason returned to his bedroll and stretched out on it once again. He was in deep thought before he realized that Tikah was right beside him. He said nothing as he watched her lay her bed beside him. She stood above him in hesitation until Jason extended his hand up to her. She took his hand and quietly lay down on the skin beside him. Jason put his arms around Tikah and kissed her lips. The unspoken passion the two of them felt for each other could no longer be denied. Jason took off his clothes and slowly removed Tikah's dress. The warmth of their bodies pressed against each other aroused Jason in a way that he never knew possible. Tikah did not resist, she gave herself completely to Jason that night.

Jason and Tikah woke up at early light. Jason held Tikah close to him and they began to make love again. No words were spoken afterwards but they both knew they were joined together from that day forward. They packed up their belongings and began making their way closer to the hills. Jason knew that the vague shadows that cut into the hills were the openings of caves. He wondered if Tikah saw them too. He remembered what she had said about going into the hills alone. It was a bad idea, but he knew that she was set in her ways. Jason remembered the light Tikah had seen the night before. Although he had not seen it for himself, he knew Tikah's young eyesight could be trusted. A light in the middle of nowhere probably meant a campfire, and a campfire meant people.

Jason shook his head and wondered, *What kind of people would be out there? Maybe a lonely hunter or maybe someone who didn't need or want company.* Jason cursed silently to himself. If only he had his gun. If only Tikah weren't insisting on going up there by herself. If only…

Tikah's voice interrupted Jason's thoughts. "You look worried. What is troubling you?"

"You can call off this whole idea of yours and come back with me," Jason said. "Stay with me. Live with me and learn my way of life."

Tikah looked into Jason's eyes and was pleased. What he was saying meant that she was special to him. She now knew he felt the same about her as she did about him. In a soft voice Tikah said, "I wish that for us, and I would like to live with you and learn your ways. But I must help my father before I can think of myself or you."

Jason stood in silence for a minute and then said, "We have been walking for a few hours now. Let's rest a while. We are almost there, but we're going to need as much strength as we can muster for the climb."

Tikah said nothing. Jason and Tikah sat down and leaned against a shady tree. Jason began to think about all that had happened in the last few weeks since he left the fort. Jason looked over at Tikah and saw that she had closed her eyes to rest. He closed his eyes too.

When Jason woke, he knew that he had slept longer than he had intended. He had wanted only to close his eyes for a few minutes and then start again toward the caves. By the position of the sun, he knew he had been asleep for over an hour. He stood up and stretched, looking casually for Tikah. He froze as he saw that she was nowhere in sight. She had often gone off by herself before, so he called to her, but there was no answer.

Damn it! he thought. *She's gone up there alone.* Jason took a hold of the travois and started walking toward the hills as fast as his legs could carry him. When he reached the hill that Tikah described during their earlier conversation about the Cave of the Great Ones, he let go of the travois and jumped one rock and then another. He began climbing a boulder, pulling himself higher toward the entrance of the cave.

When he reached the entrance, he stopped. He could hear only the sound of his fast breathing. His eyes searched the cave, but he saw nothing. His eyes were not yet adjusted to the darkness of the cave. Jason called Tikah's name, but there was no answer, only the echo of his own voice. He walked into the cave a little further and noticed something to his left. He bent down and picked it up. It was a saddlebag, and it was army-issue. He opened the bag and looked inside, but it was empty.

As his eyes adjusted to the dim light in the cave, Jason explored more of his surroundings and discovered additional items. First, he saw a canteen and a shirt, both army-issue. There were lanterns and food on the other side of him. He looked at a lantern and thought, *Probably the light Tikah saw. But where did this stuff come from?*

Deep in his thoughts, Jason didn't hear a man coming from behind. Suddenly, a thousand tiny white lights exploded in his head as he fell unconscious to the ground.

Jason woke to the sound of voices. He lay there and listened. The voices seemed muffled and far away. Slowly, he sat up, shaking his head to try to clear it. He realized his hands and feet were tied. The voices were coming closer now, but he could do nothing. His mind still cloudy, he just sat and waited. His captors soon entered.

"So you're still alive," one of them sneered at Jason.

"Who are you?" Jason asked, his vision still impaired from the sharp blow to his head.

"You don't remember me? Well, now I feel real bad about that, real bad. You're a tough one to get rid of, McIvers. I thought we'd seen the last of you back at the river."

Jason's mind came alive with the startling realization that he was face-to-face with Straton.

"Don't know how you survived that fall, being shot and all. But no matter, you're here now, and this time you won't get away," Straton continued. Straton knelt beside Jason and asked, "Why did you follow us? Was it to recover the money for that fat colonel and make yourself a big man in his eyes? Did you think that you could do that all by yourself?"

Jason's mind raced. Was Tikah in the cave too, and if so, did Straton know she was there? Jason couldn't be sure about any of this, so he decided to keep quiet about Tikah.

"Tell me something, McIvers," Straton said. "Did you come alone? I mean, you don't happen to have a bunch of army boys outside waiting for you to give the come-ahead signal now, do you?" Straton backhanded him across the face. "Well, do you?" he yelled.

"No," Jason answered. "I'm alone."

Straton stood and turned to another man behind him and said, "Check it out."

"Thought you'd be halfway to Mexico by now," Jason said to Straton.

"Now you know the colonel would have sent out a search party for us as soon as he got word that we never made it to Fort Cross. We've laid low for a while."

Jason raised an eyebrow and said, "Why did you ask me if I came alone?"

"Don't count on the cavalry, McIvers. They won't find us or you."

Jason saw the man come back from the entrance of the cave. "No one else out there, Lew. Just him."

"See that it stays that way. Get back out there and keep your eyes open," Straton replied.

The man hesitated and asked, "How much longer are we gonna have to stay holed up around here, Lew? Why can't we just take our chances and go? Let's face it. If he found us"—he pointed to Jason—"so will the army."

"Because," Straton said, "he didn't come looking for us." Straton snapped his fingers to one of the men standing off to the other side of the cave, "He came looking for her."

A man walked out of the dark shadows of the cave with Tikah.

"Our friend here has gone and got himself a squaw since we saw him last."

Jason strained against the ropes binding his hands.

"Take it easy, McIvers," said Straton. "You and your squaw here are gonna be our guests for a while, just until we see those soldier boys pass us by. After they are gone, we're on our way to Mexico."

"And then what?" Jason asked.

Straton took a step toward Jason and said, "And then, my friend, we finish what we started back at the river."

"The girl knows nothing of this," Jason said. "Let her go."

"Oh no, McIvers," Straton said. "She's comin' with us."

"You plannin' to kill her too?" Jason asked.

Straton sneered at him. "She lives for as long as she wants, providin' she does what she's told."

Again the ropes cut into Jason's wrists.

Straton laughed and turned to the man holding Tikah. "Take her down the tunnel to the rear of the cave." He turned to Jason and said, "Rest easy for now."

Jason watched Straton and Travis head off in the direction of a different tunnel from where Tikah was taken. He was alone now, and somehow, he had to get free. He scanned the area for something he could use to cut the ropes. He knew Straton would eventually kill them both.

Jason's eyes caught the lantern near the entrance of the cave. Slowly, he inched his way toward it. If he could get the ropes close enough to the flame, he could burn them off. With his back to the lantern, he moved his hands toward the flame. He could feel the heat of the flame against his wrists as he moved closer to it. As the flame burned the ropes, Jason was able to start pulling his hands apart. He flinched as the flame licked his wrists along with the fibers. He pulled harder, and the ropes gave way. Quickly, Jason's hands flew to the ropes around his ankles. He stood and tested his legs as he rubbed his wrists to speed the circulation that had been slowed by the bindings.

He started for the rear of the cave, where one of the men had taken Tikah, but his feet froze when he heard someone coming. Slowly, he backed into the shadows of the cave. He picked up a big rock and waited. As the man passed, Jason moved quickly. He raised the rock, and with all his might he struck the man on the head. The man fell with a groan and was still. Jason checked, and the man was dead. He grabbed the man's gun and shoved it in his belt. He would have to act fast now.

Jason ran toward the rear of the cave, checking every tunnel along the way. He came to a turn and edged slowly around it. Upon turning, he saw Tikah sitting quietly. A man was sitting in front of her with his rifle lying across his lap. He was resting lightly, almost dozing, but he was not asleep. Tikah saw Jason, and her eyes warned him of the man guarding her. Jason eased the gun from his belt and cocked it. The man heard the sound and stood up, startled to see Jason standing over him.

With the gun pointed at the man's face, Jason said in a low voice, "Stand easy, mister, and throw the rifle this way."

The man did what he was told. Jason turned to Tikah. "Hurry—we haven't got much time."

She got up and moved toward Jason. Jason said to Tikah, "Get the rifle."

She bent to pick it up. At the same time the man suddenly lunged toward Jason and tried to take the gun away from him. It was a short struggle before the gun went off and the man fell to the ground.

"Damn it," Jason said. "That shot will bring them back here." Jason grabbed the lantern and the rifle and then took Tikah's arm. Together they ran deeper into the caves. It was their only hope of hiding from Straton.

"Wait, listen." Jason cocked an ear. "Sounds like gunfire at the front of the cave. Let's go back," Jason said.

Tikah did not want to move. She said, "No, they will find us. They already know we have escaped."

But Jason was insistent. "Listen to those shots." Jason's mind clicked. "Maybe it's the army! Straton said they hadn't passed here yet, and if it is, we don't want to get caught back here."

Tikah nodded in silent agreement, and they began making their way back to the entrance of the cave.

Jason's hunch had been right. At the entrance of the cave, he could see Straton, firing outward. He also could see the blue line of soldiers from where he stood, firing back. Straton had the saddlebag with the money in it close to his feet.

Jason motioned for Tikah to stay back around the corner in one of the tunnels. He cocked the gun and said, "Don't move, Straton."

Straton turned to face Jason. "Figured you'd get away, but it's no use. One of my men is on your left, and his gun is pointed right at your back."

Jason turned and saw Travis pointing a gun at him, so he tossed his gun aside, and Travis picked it up.

"Now," Straton continued, "you and the girl are going to get us out of here." Straton shouted to Travis, "Cover him!" Then he turned to face the entrance of the cave. "Hey, soldiers, hold your fire. I got me some hostages here. Let us come down and ride out of here, or they die."

A voice from below answered, "No deals. Just let them go."

Straton thought for a while and then turned to Travis and said, "Get the dynamite."

Travis tossed Straton a stick of dynamite. Straton lit it and hurled it toward the soldiers below. He laughed as he watched the men scatter just before it exploded.

"Now I mean business!" Straton yelled. "Back off, or you'll all die."

He was answered by a volley of gunfire that cost Straton his last man, Travis. Straton was alone now. Straton reached for another stick of dynamite and lit it as Jason went for Travis's gun. At the same time, another volley of bullets entered the cave. Jason took cover. A bullet nicked Straton's wrist, causing him to drop the dynamite, which rolled toward the box of unlit dynamite. Jason saw his chance. He lunged toward Straton, hitting him hard. As they fought, they lost their balance and fell out of the cave and onto the ledge just below the entrance. Jason had Straton by the throat as Straton clung to the saddlebag with the money still in it.

Jason looked toward the entrance of the cave just as a large explosion went off. The entrance of the cave completely collapsed, and the force of the explosion caused Jason and Straton to fall to the ground below. Straton died from the fall. Weakly, Jason tried to stand, aware of blood oozing from his body. He saw two men in uniform at his side.

"Easy, mister," someone said.

Jason pointed a shaky finger toward the cave and said, "Tikah. I've got to …"

"Lay still, mister," said a voice. "He's in bad shape, Captain."

The captain instructed the men, "Get him on a horse, and be careful."

Jason fought against their assistance and said, "No … got to get back to the cave … got to get back." Jason felt himself drifting further away. The voices around him grew faint, and soon he heard nothing; he felt nothing as he slipped into unconsciousness.

CHAPTER 5

Jason lay motionless and near death as Colonel Ashby's personal medic tended to him, with not much hope for Jason's recovery.

"He's in bad shape, Colonel," the medic said.

"Do whatever you can to save this man's life," the colonel said. "I owe him a lot. He brought Straton and his men to the justice they deserved, and he saved my daughter's dowry. Can you make out what he keeps saying?"

"I don't know. He keeps repeating something that sounds like 'Tikah,'" the medic replied.

A few more days passed before Jason woke to find himself bathed, bandaged up, and lying between clean, fresh white sheets. As he tried to clear the cobwebs from his head, he wondered what had happened and where he was. Then suddenly, he bolted up as if he had been hit by lightning and yelled, "Tikah!"

The medic came running into the room and quickly put his hands on Jason's shoulders. "Hold on there, fella.

You ain't in no shape to be moving around." Turning away from Jason, he shouted, "Get the colonel!"

Colonel Ashby quickly came into the room and said, "Welcome back, McIvers! We weren't sure you were going to make it."

"How long have I been here?" Jason asked.

"Going on a week now," the medic answered.

"A week!" Jason shouted. He tried to get up, but his legs failed.

"Hold on, McIvers!" the colonel shouted. "What's your dad-gum hurry? You darn near died."

"Tikah!" Jason replied.

"Yeah, I was meanin' to ask you about that. Ever since the explosion at that cave, you have been saying 'Tikah.' What is Tikah?"

"It's not what, Colonel; it's who! I would not be alive today if not for Tikah. She is an Indian girl who found me after Straton and his men tried to kill me. It was a setup all along, Colonel. Straton and his men are the ones who robbed the payroll detail, and Straton was the mastermind behind the whole dowry robbery. They shot me and left me for dead. But I escaped. I was hurt bad, but Tikah found me and nursed me back to health."

"We knew something was wrong when we got word that Lieutenant Straton and you never made it to Fort Cross. We figured it was Indians, same as with the payroll detail," Colonel Ashby said.

"No Indians, Colonel," Jason said. "It was Straton all along. He and his men made it look like Indians by shootin' everybody with arrows. I saw the bow and arrows in a pouch on Travis's saddle, and they were going to do the same thing to me—make it look like we were attacked by Indians."

"Yes," the colonel said, "my men saw them too when they found Straton's horses hidden away. How could I have been so wrong about someone? And to think, I trusted him with my daughter's dowry and asked him to stand up for me at my daughter's wedding. Dad-gum fool!"

"When can I get out of this bed?" Jason asked. "I got to go find Tikah."

"Not so quick there, McIvers," the colonel said. "You won't be no good to her or anyone else right now with the shape you're in. When you are better, we'll send along a detail with you, and you can find this girl Tikah, if she wants to be found."

Jason lay back down, weak and exhausted. He closed his eyes and quickly fell asleep.

Jason got stronger and stronger with each passing day. Soon he would be able to ride out of the fort and head back to the cave where he had last seen Tikah. He could not bear the thought of losing her. *She has to be alive. She has to be*, Jason thought.

"Good morning, McIvers," the medic said as he joined Jason, who was sitting out on the porch. "Mighty fine day."

"Yes, it is," Jason said. "Look, Doc, I gotta get out of here. I gotta get back to the cave. Tikah may still be alive, and she needs me."

"Well, I'm not in favor of you traveling right yet, but I know there won't be no holdin' you back for much longer," the medic replied as he got up and went inside.

Just then, the gate at the front of the fort opened, and a lone rider trotted in. The man was familiar to Jason;

Jason had seen him around the fort in the past, but he didn't know him. It was a strange thing—this young man wasn't white, and he wasn't Indian. He dressed somewhat like an Indian but mostly like a cowhand. He was darker than a typical white man, probably from exposure to the sun. He didn't have the features of an Indian, but he did have an Indian look about him.

The man rode up to where Jason was sitting and dismounted. He was tying up his horse when his eyes met Jason's. "Howdy," he said.

Jason returned the greeting with a nod and asked, "Where you from, boy?"

The young man said, "My name is Clayton, but the tribe out east of here calls me Pale One."

"Well," Jason said, "mind if I call you Clayton?"

"Go right ahead," Clayton said. "I've been called a lot worse. What name do you go by?"

"McIvers, Jason McIvers. What brings you to the fort?" Jason asked.

"Supplies. I need to stock up with enough food and water for a long, hard three days' ride I'm planning."

"Where you headed, Clayton?" Jason asked.

"You wouldn't know of it. It's a cave, a sacred place."

Jason's heart raced, and he sat up as if he had been bitten by a fire ant. "Tell me about this cave. And what does it mean to you?" Jason said while trying not to act too excited.

"It's called the Cave of the Great Ones. It is a place where the spirits of chiefs from the tribe go when they enter the afterworld. Their spirits forever ride with the Great Ones."

Jason's heart raced as Clayton spoke. *Tikah*, he thought. *This man is from Tikah's tribe.* But Jason held his tongue for a while longer while Clayton continued his story.

"There is a girl from our tribe who has gone missing, and I got to find her. She's special to me. There is a custom to not speak the name of a Great One who has passed on for the time it takes the moon to go from one full moon to another. Her father, the chief of our tribe, died gloriously in battle against the Hokawa tribe. And one night he came to Tikah in a dream. Overwhelmed with love and joy, she said his name in her sleep. Her mother heard her speak his name and told the others. Because of that, she was cast out."

"Does this girl have a name?" Jason asked.

"Tikah. Her name is Tikah," Clayton said.

Jason could hardly contain his emotions but decided to keep his feelings hidden for a while longer.

Clayton continued, "I know in my heart Tikah went to the Cave of the Great Ones to beg forgiveness of the gods for her slip of the tongue and to beg for the chief's spirit to be allowed to ride for all eternity with the Great Ones. But she never returned. I fear something happened, and I have to find her."

Jason decided not to tell Clayton that he knew Tikah and her story until he learned more about this man called Clayton and what he meant to Tikah. "It's a hard three days' ride out there and back. Nothin' between here and there except a lot of heat and dust," Jason said. "Guess we should get an early start in the morning."

"We?" Clayton said. "I ride alone."

With Jason's urgency to find out what had happened to Tikah, he was not going to take no for an answer.

"Look, Clayton," Jason said, "I been holed up at this fort for too dang long. Time for me to ride out. Besides, what's the harm in having someone to ride along with?" Jason hoped Clayton would not object. He had to go. He had to find out what had happened to Tikah.

"Well," Clayton said, "just so you know, I can go it alone, but I guess I can't stop you from ridin' along if you want."

Jason was relieved and said, "Good. Then we'll ride out early tomorrow."

The night was long, and Jason didn't sleep a wink, wondering about Tikah. So many questions were racing through his mind. Was she still alive? Who was this man Clayton to her? Would she be happy to see him? Would Tikah still want to live with Jason and learn his ways liked they'd talked about? What about her quest to make peace with the gods? Would her father, the great chief of her tribe, be granted the honor of riding with the Great Ones for all eternity? Jason was tormented all night and was happy to see the sun rise.

Jason loaded up his provisions and went to see the colonel before he left. "Morning, Colonel," Jason said.

"Morning, son. You're lookin' mighty fine. How you feelin'?" the colonel asked.

"I feel good, Colonel," Jason said. "Just stoppin' by to let you know that I'll be ridin' out this morning."

"Where you headed, son?" the colonel asked.

"I'm ridin' out with Clayton," Jason said.

"You mean Pale One?" the colonel asked. "What's your business with him?"

"He knows Tikah. He knows she went to the cave, and he is going to go and find her," Jason said.

"How? How does he know about all that?" the colonel asked.

Jason answered, "He's from the Opoka tribe, Tikah's tribe! He said she is special to him, and I gotta find out more. Most of all, I gotta find out if she is still alive."

"You mean you didn't tell him you know Tikah or how you were there at the cave with her?" the colonel asked.

"No, sir. And I ain't gonna say anything about it for now, not until I find out more about him and what he means to Tikah."

"All right," the colonel said. "You want a detail to ride along with you?"

"No," Jason answered. "Clayton—or Pale One—didn't even want me ridin' with him. We'll go alone."

"Have it your way," the colonel said. "Just be careful out there. If there is anything you need, just say so. I'm beholden to you."

"Thanks, Colonel," Jason said. "I'll be on my way." Through the windows of the colonel's office, Jason could see that Clayton was mounted and ready to go. Jason tipped his hat at the colonel and said, "Thanks for everything, Colonel, and thank your medic for me too."

With that, Jason turned and walked out the door. The colonel watched through the window as Jason mounted his horse and the two men rode out of the fort. The gate closed quickly behind them.

CHAPTER 6

The sun was just coming up over the ridge as Jason and Clayton rode off toward the hills. It would be a hard day's ride ahead of them before their first stop.

About an hour before nightfall, they decided it was time to stop and make camp. They had covered a lot of miles on their first day, and they were right where they wanted to be after one day's ride. The scenery looked all too familiar to Jason. He knew they were headed in the right direction to the cave. He thought about how much easier the trek was with a horse and plenty of provisions.

"I'll get a fire started," Clayton said.

Jason picked a nice spot for his bedroll and piled up some leaves and brush to cushion the ground below it.

Night fell quickly. After Jason heated supper over the campfire, the two men lay back on their bedrolls, with their saddles serving as pillows. Jason gazed up to the clear sky and stared at all the stars twinkling above. There was a steady song of crickets in the distance. The fire crackled next to him, and the embers popped in the darkness.

Once again, Jason's mind wandered to Tikah. Was she alive? Jason's curiosity overcame him, and he had to ask Clayton, "How is it that you came to know Tikah?"

There was a long pause before Clayton said, "It was many years ago. I was just a boy, not much more than five or six. We were traveling across the land, headed west. The wagon train was not long, and I remember my mother and father saying how happy they were about starting our new life out west. Our families all knew each other well, and there were plenty of kids for my brother and me to play with. The trip was hard—long dusty days and short cold nights. Felt like we were always moving and not sleeping much. Talk was it was safer to keep moving than it was to dally."

Jason reached over to get another cup of coffee as Clayton continued.

"Everything was going along fine. We had no trouble—no sickness, no lame horses, and no wagons broke down. If there was any trouble, us kids didn't know about it. Then one night, after we were done traveling for the day and the wagons were circled, we settled in for the night. Everybody began to light their campfires and fix supper. After supper, sometime before dusk, there was an eerie sound off in the distance. It was a sound that I will never forget. It sounded like a hundred horses' hooves galloping on the dry prairie at a fast pace toward us. We could hear screaming, and I saw dust rising from the ground up to the air as the sun started to set. My father grabbed me and put me in a hiding place under the floorboard of the wagon. He covered me with a blanket and told me not to move. I don't know where my brother hid, but I was alone. I closed my eyes and covered my ears as the sound got louder and louder. I heard gunfire coming from all around me. I heard screaming from the Indians outside the wagon circle and screaming from my mother and the others inside the circle."

Clayton spoke as if he were deep in a trance, almost as if he were reliving the whole attack again. "I don't know how long this lasted—when you're a child, time goes by slow—but soon there was silence from within the wagon circle. I didn't move. I lay there under the blanket and waited for my father to come for me, but he never did. Soon I could hear voices, but they did not speak English. They were all around. It sounded like they were going from wagon to wagon, taking what they wanted. I know this because I felt the movement of the wagon I was hiding in as two men jumped in. I could hear them smashing our belongings and throwing things all around, looking for whatever they wanted to steal. After what seemed like a long time, I heard the sound of horses galloping away, more horses than what had come—I think they took our horses too. And then it was quiet. They were gone. I still did not move. I still waited for my father, and he still did not come. I don't remember much after that."

"Yep, Indian raid," Jason said.

With eyes fixed on the campfire, Clayton said, "Yes. It was the Hokawa tribe."

"I think I've heard of them. They are a vicious group," Jason said.

"They are a renegade tribe with no values—no respect for Mother Earth, no respect for the gods or for life at all," replied Clayton. "They do not work for what is theirs; they steal. They steal from the white man and make war on other Indian tribes. I know this because I was told of the evil ways of the Hokawa tribe by Tikah's family."

"How is it you ended up with Tikah and her tribe?" Jason interrupted.

Again, there was a long pause before Clayton answered. "I don't know how long I stayed under the floorboard of the wagon, but I was found by Tikah's father, great chief of the Opoka tribe. I was little, and I was scared, but the Great One thought my people meant his people no harm. He could see that I had been left all alone, so he allowed me to stay with the tribe and learn their ways. He called me 'Pale One.' The women of the tribe took care of me. I was not treated as an outcast because of the color of my skin. But there was always a certain distance between me and them. I was a white boy; I would never grow up to be an Indian warrior."

Jason finished the last few sips of his coffee and put his cup down on the rocks encircling the fire. He lay back on his bedroll as Clayton continued.

"I never knew what happened to my mother and father or my brother or anyone else traveling in our wagon train. Tikah was about my age. Children know nothing about other children—they are all the same to each other—and she became my friend very soon. You could say we grew up together. Most of what I know about the Indian ways, she taught me. She taught me to speak their language, and I taught her how to speak mine."

So that is how she knew English, Jason thought.

"We spent a lot of time together. I grew very fond of her and even thought that maybe someday we would marry and have a family of our own. But it was forbidden by the Great One. It is their custom to marry only their own kind. She would never get permission from the Great One to marry a white man. I knew that, but just to be near her meant so much to me. We have a bond between us that cannot be broken."

After another long moment of silence Jason said, "Well, I guess we better get some shut-eye."

Jason did not say anything more. He lay there looking up at the stars and thought, *Tikah belongs to another man. How can this be? How did we grow so close in such a short time if her heart belongs to Pale One? How is it that we lay in each other's arms and slept as one if she belonged to someone else? Being with her was the best thing that has ever happened to this miserable ole lonely trapper.* Jason couldn't make sense of it. He closed his eyes but lay there a long time before he fell asleep.

Clayton woke to the smell of coffee coming from the campfire. "Morning, Jason," Clayton said. "Sleep well?" he asked.

Jason lied, "Yep, like a baby." He didn't want to let on how devastated he had been to hear that Tikah belonged to Clayton. He poured himself a cup of coffee and said, "Better pack up soon. We got another long day's ride ahead of us."

It was another hot and dusty day along the way, no different from the day before. Jason and Clayton stopped a couple of times to rest in the shade, drink some water, and wet their dry lips before continuing on.

Clayton noticed how quiet Jason was but thought this was probably just his way.

Jason tried to think of something to say, but he was too overcome with sadness. He told himself he would have to let Tikah go. It wasn't right for a man to come between another man and his woman.

The second day's ride was about to come to an end. Clayton spotted a good place to set up camp and asked Jason, "You about done for the day?"

Jason replied, "Yep, I reckon so. This is as good a place as any."

The men dismounted and tied up their horses. Each did his part to set up camp for the night.

Jason began to warm some meat in the pot. "There's enough here for the two of us if you're interested," Jason said. "I also got some potatoes that I brought from the fort that I can throw in."

"Sounds good," Clayton said. "Mighty nice of you."

Again, Jason was quiet while the two of them ate their supper. But Clayton finally got him to talk a little when he asked, "What do you do to get by, Jason?"

Jason replied, "I'm a trapper. Been doing it all my life. Pretty much all I know."

"Must be lonely work," Clayton said.

"Yep, it is. I stay out in the woods for about six months at a time, tendin' my traps, and when I have enough furs piled up, I take them to the fort and sell them. Then I usually spend what I make in Ike's Saloon, get in a fight, and bust the place up a little, which sometimes lands me in the guardhouse till I sleep it off. Most times I pay for the damages and head on out in the morning and don't go back for another six months."

"You don't have a woman at home?" Clayton asked.

Jason threw the last few drops of his coffee into the fire. The fire hissed as the coffee hit the flames. "Nope," he said. "There was a woman once, but she's gone now. I have a cabin set up just fine for myself. I have everything I need there to get by. I'm used to being alone."

Probably why he don't talk much, Clayton thought. "Well, sounds like you found your way of life that seems to suit you, but for me, I would rather have the company of a woman like Tikah. I am grateful to the tribe for taking me in after I lost my family. I don't know what would have become of me had that not happened."

"Interesting how life is sometimes," Jason said. "I think I'm going to get some shut-eye now."

"Yes, me too," Clayton said. "Ya know, Jason, I'm glad you're here."

"Me too," Jason said before rolling over.

Morning came along fast, and both men were eager to get back on the trail. Their ride together was almost over, and they both were thinking about Tikah and wondering if she would still be alive.

Jason toyed with the notion of telling Clayton about himself and Tikah but then thought, *What would be the point? Tikah belongs to Clayton.* It would be a mistake to believe things would be any different if she were still alive. But there was still the time he and Tikah had had together. The memory of her and the nights they had spent together would last him the rest of his life. Jason didn't know what he would do if they did find Tikah alive.

They were almost to the foothills of the cave. Jason did not know how he would explain how he knew which cave to go to when Clayton did not know. There were many caves in that area. All Clayton knew was the legend of the Cave of the Great Ones. He had never been there and had not told the others that he was going. All he knew was that the cave was a large one and sat at the top of a long climb up a steep rock ridge.

Come morning, Jason and Clayton would know what had become of Tikah.

CHAPTER 7

The two men rode up to the tall rock ridge. Clayton could see many caves far above the rocks but had no idea which cave was the mythical Cave of the Great Ones. The men got off their horses and tied them to a nearby tree. They quickly began to climb the steep rocks and large boulders. About halfway up, a rock gave way under Clayton's foot, and he watched it fall to the ground far below him.

When they reached the plateau where Jason and Straton had fought about two weeks ago, Jason saw that the entrance of the cave was completely collapsed. There were rocks and debris all around.

"Must have been a cave-in at some time," Clayton said as he made his way toward another cave.

Without thinking, Jason said excitedly, "No! This is the cave!"

Clayton stopped to look back at Jason and said, "What makes you so sure this is the one? Nothing would able to get in or out of this cave."

Jason realized he had almost let on that he knew about this place. He had to think of something to say and say it quick. "Just a hunch I got. Don't ask me how, but my gut tells me this is the one."

Clayton thought Jason was acting strange, but he decided to turn and go back to the cave entrance. Jason had already begun removing rocks and rubble. Clayton stood next to him and helped. They worked for close to an hour before any real progress could be seen, but they were getting closer to opening it up, so much so that Jason yelled, "Tikah! Are you in there?"

Clayton did the same. "Tikah! Can you hear me?"

But there was only silence.

Jason and Clayton continued to dig away at the rubble until Jason felt that they were just about ready to break through. He stood back a moment. His heart was racing. Sweat was dripping off both men from their fast, furious work to clear an opening. This was what they had ridden so far for. This was about to give them the answer they were both looking for.

Clayton took over in the spot where Jason had been digging and continued to call for Tikah. "Tikah! Can you hear me? Are you in there?"

But still there was no response.

Clayton began to doubt Jason's gut feeling that this was the right cave and said to Jason, "This is crazy. Nothing or no one is in this cave."

But Jason argued, "Keep digging! This is the cave! I know it is!"

So Clayton kept digging, and soon he was able to open a small hole to peek inside. He could not see a thing in the darkness behind all the rocks and rubble, but soon the hole was big enough for him to put his arm through. Clayton shouted again, "Tikah! Can you hear me? Are you in there?"

And as if hit by a bolt of lightning, Clayton felt a small, cold hand touch his hand. "Tikah!" he yelled. "Hold on—I'm here. Tikah! You're alive!"

Clayton and Jason dug harder and faster at the opening, and soon Clayton was able to crawl through the hole and into the cave. There he saw Tikah lying on the cave floor, weak, frightened, and timid but alive, barely. Clayton crawled over to Tikah and put his arms around her. With tears in his eyes, he said, "Tikah! You're alive! Jason, you were right! This is the right cave. Jason!"

Clayton looked back for Jason, but he was not there. Clayton again called out for him, but Jason did not answer. Clayton turned back to Tikah and saw that she was unconscious. He held her close in his arms and said again, "Hold on, Tikah. I'm here. You are safe now. I'll take care of you. It will be okay." Clayton rocked back and forth while he held Tikah in his arms.

Tikah opened her eyes, but Clayton could tell that she was not fully conscious. She looked all around until her eyes met his. She stared into his eyes in disbelief and said, "Pale One, is it really you?"

"Yes!" Clayton said. "Yes, it's me. I am happy you are alive. I have come far to find you, and I am so grateful that we found you alive!"

"How?" Tikah said. "How did you find me? How did you know where to look?"

"A man rode with me. I only met him a few days ago,

but he insisted on riding with me. I told him about my journey to find you. He knew of the caves and brought me to this place."

"What man?" Tikah asked.

"It's not important now," Clayton said. "Besides, he's gone. What's important is that I found you and you're alive!"

Tikah closed her eyes and was happy to feel Pale One's arms around her. She knew she would be safe. She knew she would soon get out of this cave and return to her people. She hoped that her mother would welcome her back.

As Clayton rocked Tikah in his arms, he couldn't help but wonder, *What happened here?* Nothing made sense. He wondered, *Is this even the Cave of the Great Ones?*

He saw items scattered all over the cave, but they were not items that a great Indian warrior would have. These were white men's things. How had they gotten there? Everything bore the mark of the army. He saw food, water, bedrolls, picks and shovels, and medical supplies—enough supplies to last a month or more. *How did all these supplies get here?* Clayton wondered.

Well, it's not important now, he thought. *Important thing is to get a fire going and get some hot food for Tikah!* He gently laid Tikah down and covered her with one of the blankets to keep her warm.

He built a fire from wood that he found scattered all over the cave. He moved more rocks and rubble away from the cave entrance to allow light and fresh air to enter. Then he saw a dead white man lying off to the side in the shadows. Clayton wondered, *What terrible things happened here? Poor Tikah, what did she suffer through?*

Once the fire was well established, Clayton moved the dead man's body out of the cave and onto the ledge below the entrance. Then he began to search through the cave and gather what he could find to make Tikah comfortable. Among the army supplies he found ingredients to fix a broth with small pieces of dried meat in it over the campfire. *Don't want to give her too much yet, not knowing how long it's been since she last ate*, he thought.

When the food was ready, Clayton helped Tikah sit up a little and fed her some broth and meat. She smiled as she sipped the broth and tasted the meat, and that made Clayton happy.

"Are you hurt?" Clayton asked. "Anything broke?"

"I don't think so," Tikah said in a soft, weak voice.

"Good, good," Clayton said. "Just lie back and rest for now. This will all be over soon."

By now it was dark outside, and Tikah was resting comfortably. Clayton stoked the fire a little and lay down on a bedroll he'd found in the cave. All of Clayton's belongings were still with his horse far below them.

Wonder what happened to Jason, he thought. *Awful strange for him to just up and disappear like that after traveling so far and working so hard to open the cave. Mighty strange.*

Clayton looked over at Tikah and saw that she was sleeping peacefully. He closed his eyes and fell right to sleep.

Clayton didn't know how long he had been asleep when the rays of the sun shone through the cave entrance. He looked over at Tikah and saw that she was beginning to stir. He got up to put another piece of wood on the fire and to get something more for them to eat from the army provisions he'd found earlier.

Behind him, he heard a soft, weak voice say, "Good morning, Pale One!"

That was great to hear, and Clayton quickly turned and said right back, "Good morning, Tikah! How are you feeling?"

Tikah answered, "I am well. I have been well cared for! How long have I been here?"

Clayton said, "Not sure. Many, many days."

"Pale One," Tikah said, "I spoke to the council of the great chiefs. They came to me in my darkest time alone here in the cave. I begged their forgiveness and asked that my father be granted the honor to ride with the Great Ones. I told them of my dream and how in my sleep I said my father's name when the mourning period was not yet over. I told them I was not even aware that I had spoken his name, and they told me that they knew of my words. And then, when I felt my end was near, and I was to die all alone in this cave, my father appeared before me.

"He was standing with the Great Ones, looking strong. He was a proud warrior once again, and he spoke to me. He told me that I need to be strong. He told me that I have a long life ahead to live. He said that I should not be troubled about this any longer. The Great Ones have made peace with me. Then he told me it was time for me to go back among the living. And at that moment I felt your hand in mine. It was my father's will that I should live."

"Tikah, do you think your father was giving his consent for you and me to live as one?" Clayton asked.

"Do you think that was his way of giving our union his blessing, telling you that it no longer matters to him that I am a white man on the outside, for he now knows that what is inside tells him that I am Opoka, worthy of the gift of his daughter?"

"I don't know what to think of any of this, Pale One," Tikah said. "All I know is that my father will ride with the Great Ones for all eternity, and that makes me very happy."

"I think we have talked enough for now," Clayton said. "Get some rest, and we will talk of this again soon."

Tikah rolled over and closed her eyes. She was happy about her father but sad about what might have become of Jason. *Why did he not come for me?* she wondered. *Something must have happened to him.*

Tikah knew how Jason felt about her, and she was happy about it. She felt the same for him, and even though it was forbidden for her to marry someone not of her kind, she had been willing to give up her life with the Opoka people to be with Jason. She had never felt so safe and so loved before she met Jason.

I know Pale One has feelings for me, and I love him very much, she thought, *but not the love one feels for a husband, but instead more like a brother. We grew up together, and we are very close, but we have never been as close as Jason and I were while lying together under the stars. Jason is the only man that I have given myself to. I have to find out what happened to him. I cannot speak of this to Pale One. It would hurt him. But someday he must know that I have given my body and soul to Jason. It is Jason I wish to be with, only Jason.*

Sleep quickly overcame her.

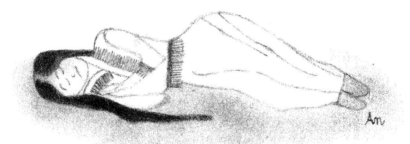

CHAPTER 8

Tikah woke a while later to the sound of Clayton moving around in the cave. She could see that he had gathered up many things from all around.

"There are enough supplies here to last us all the way back to our people and then some," Clayton said to Tikah. "How do you suppose all these things got here?"

Tikah, not wanting to speak of Jason yet, left him out of her answer. She said, "On my way up the ridge to the Cave of the Great Ones, I did not know there was anyone in the cave. Even after I made it to the top and entered the cave, I could see no one else inside. I sat and rested for a while. I could see that the cave went far back into the mountain, with many tunnels leading to other caverns deeper in the mountain. I got up and started to move deeper into the cave using only the light that shined in from the entrance. As I got further back into the cave, I began to hear voices, white men's voices.

"I thought to myself, I am in the wrong cave, for the voices I hear should be those of the Opoka tongue. And just then, a man came around the corner and saw me. I quickly turned to run, but he was quicker than I, and he grabbed me. I remember he said, 'Well, lookie here, boys, we got ourselves an Injun squaw.' I tried to break free, but his grip was too powerful. They did not know that I can speak the words of the white man, and I did not let them believe different. There are many happenings that I cannot remember." She thought again about Jason but continued to leave him out of the story.

"But I came to know that one of these men was from the army fort. He and his men had robbed a group of soldiers who were bringing money to the fort and had made it look like Indians did it. The man from the fort and the others were hiding here from the soldiers. They were going to ride to Mexico as soon as they were sure the soldiers were not following them. I don't think they knew they were in the sacred Cave of the Great Ones."

"They did not hurt you, did they?" Clayton asked. "They did not ... you know, have their way with you, did they?"

"No, Pale One, they did not," Tikah answered, "but the man from the fort decided it was time for them to leave, and they were going to take me with them to be their squaw. I heard them say they would have their way with me when the time came."

Clayton was relieved to hear that Tikah had not been harmed or soiled. She was still pure, and he delighted in that. Tikah knew that this was what Clayton was thinking and that he would be sickened if he learned that another man had taken her, especially in a violent way.

She couldn't help but wonder how Pale One would

react if he knew the truth about her and Jason. *Maybe it will be better for him not to know*, she thought.

"So how is it that you got trapped in the cave?" Clayton asked.

Tikah began again, careful not to mention Jason. "About the time the men were gathering their belongings, they realized that the soldiers from the fort were here and had them cornered in the cave. A gunfight began, and most of the men were killed. Soon the man from the fort let go of me, and I ran far back into the cave. I ran and ran until I could not see light any longer. I slid my hands along the walls of the cave, and I ran blindly. I was running as far away as I could go when all of a sudden, there was a big noise. The sound thundered through the whole mountainside. I have never heard anything as loud as that noise. I don't know how far back I was into the mountainside, but I stayed there. I did not move for a long time."

"So that is how the cave entrance got blocked off," Clayton said. "I figured it was probably a cave-in of some sort."

Tikah continued, "When I felt it was safe to go back toward the front of the cave, I listened for voices, but there were none. I kept sliding my hands along the cave walls while I walked back toward the front of the cave. I was in complete darkness. I kept thinking that light would shine into the cave soon if I just kept walking closer to the front, but the light never came. When I reached the opening of the cave where the light once was, there was only darkness. In my haste to get to where I thought the cave opening should be, I tripped over many things scattered all around. One thing I tripped on was a light box; I heard them call it a lantern earlier. I remembered seeing one of the men start the light when he took me far back into the cave. The white men had fire sticks. The man from the fort took a fire stick out of a shirt pocket lying on the ground and gave it to the other man to strike on the wall. The shirt had the army's mark on it. I knew if I could find that shirt, I would find the fire sticks and bring light into the cave."

After a pause, Tikah said, "I crawled all around the cave, feeling with my hands in all directions, until I finally felt the cloth of a shirt. It was not where I had expected it to be. I found the pocket with the fire sticks, and I was able to light the lantern as I saw them do earlier. At first my eyes hurt from the bright flame, and for the first time I saw the prison I was entombed in. I felt that I must rest for a while, then try to free myself from the cave. I sat down to rest and looked all around. I thought about how hungry and weak I felt. But rest was all my body would allow.

"I don't know how long I slept, but when I woke, I felt the hunger and weakness once again. The lantern was still lit, but I was not sure how long the light would last. I had to search quickly before the light went dark. I was able to find some of the white man's food, and I ate it hesitantly. It was not to my liking, but it did stop the hunger pains in my stomach. I was careful to keep the fire sticks close in case the lantern's flicker died. I thought that I should not light a campfire, as I was closed in with no place for the smoke to escape. And then one day, as I feared, the lantern went dark, and it would not light again. I used the last few fire sticks trying to light it. I lay there in complete darkness. I do not know how long I lay there, maybe a couple of days, thinking that this was the end of my life's journey. This was where I would die. And then the Great Ones stood before me, and I spoke with them, and my father spoke to me. That is all that I remember until I reached out and found your hand in the darkness."

"Well, you are safe now," Clayton said. "In another day or two, you will be strong enough, and we will leave this place. It is a long ride back to our people, and winter is coming."

Tikah smiled and lay back to rest. Her mind wandered, and she immediately thought about Jason. What had become of him? How long could she keep his memory and her love for him a secret?

Two more days passed, and Tikah felt strong. She and Clayton decided it was time to start their long journey home. As Tikah looked out beyond the cave's entrance, she felt the cold, crisp air outside. The leaves on the trees were a golden color, and they rained slowly down to the ground.

"You were right. Winter is coming," she said.

"Yes, I can feel the coolness in the air. We better get started."

As they began their descent down from the cave, Tikah saw on the ledge the decomposing body of the man the other white men had called Travis. Clayton warned her to look away.

Clayton found a rope among the army man's belongings. He tied one end of the rope around his waist and the other around Tikah. She started down the cliff first as Clayton kept a tight hold on the rope. Clayton thought, *If she slips, I will be tied to her, so she will not fall to the ground. A person could die falling from this place.*

It was a long, slow climb down, but they made it to the ground safely. Clayton found his horse in fine shape. There had been plenty of grass around for him to eat. Clayton noticed a small pail of water that his horse had drunk from. This seemed odd to Clayton for a moment, but he was so totally focused on Tikah that he did not give it a second thought.

He untied his horse and mounted it with one swift movement. He reached down, took a hold of Tikah's hand, and pulled her up behind him. She wrapped her arms around Clayton's waist and put her cheek on his back as they trotted off.

Tikah closed her eyes and envisioned herself riding off with Jason.

Clayton had a smile on his face and thought about what the future would bring for him and Tikah.

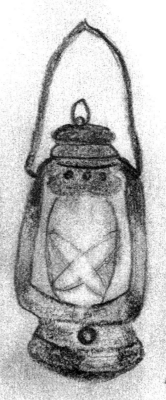

CHAPTER 9

Jason could see the fort in the distance. It was a familiar sight to him, only this time he was going to the fort empty-handed. He had no pelts to sell. Instead he was going to make a quick stop to pick up some provisions to last him through the winter. The weather was changing fast, and he knew it was time to get back home and start trapping. It also was time to shake off the memory of Tikah, and trapping would keep his mind busy.

Jason heard the soldier standing high up in the guard tower yell down, "Rider comin'!"

The gate opened, and he quickly trotted through before the gate closed right behind him. Jason decided to skip Ike's Saloon and go see the colonel instead. He tied his horse up at the hitching post just outside Colonel Ashby's office. He took his hat off and slapped at his legs with it to clean some of the dust off his pants and boots before going inside.

"Where is everybody?" Jason hollered as he walked through the outer door.

The door to the colonel's office opened, and a voice said, "Hold on, mister. I'm comin'." When Sergeant Emory came through the doorway and saw Jason, he said, "Jason, is that you? You ole son of a gun. We wasn't expectin' to see you back so soon."

Jason answered, "Yeah, it's me. Just comin' in to get some supplies to take back with me."

"You ain't gonna bust up Ike's place again, are ya?" Sergeant Emory asked.

"Nah," Jason said. "Just comin' to get some supplies. Is the colonel around?"

"He should be back shortly; he's down at the telegraph office. We've been gettin' word of some sort of an Indian uprising up north. You hear anything about it?" Sergeant Emory asked.

"No, nothing," Jason replied.

Just then the door opened, and Colonel Ashby walked in. He saw Jason standing there. With a grin on his face, the colonel walked up to Jason to shake his hand. "Well, I'll be. What brings you back here so soon?" the colonel asked. Then he turned to Sergeant Emory and said, "That will be all, Sergeant."

After the sergeant left the room, Colonel Ashby turned to Jason and gave him a big hug and a slap on the back. "Mighty fine to see you, son. Did you find that girl you were lookin' for?" he asked.

"Ah, I was just chasin' the wind, Colonel. Ain't much to tell," Jason said. "What's this I hear about an Indian uprising up north?"

"Yeah, we've been gettin' word about the Hokawas stirrin' up trouble with the other tribes. With the new settlements of folks from back east springin' up all around, I have to send out a few details to check up on them every once in a while. Those folks are mighty worried. So far there has been no trouble. Seems to be just a rift between the tribes. Hey, have you eaten?"

"No, sir," Jason replied. "Just came in off the prairie and rode straight here."

"Fine. Then let's go to Ellie's place and get some grub. Bet you could use a good home-cooked meal after being out on the trail so long. I'm buyin'. Miss Ellie makes the best biscuits you'll ever eat."

"Well, Colonel, I'm mighty sick of beans and jerky. I think I will take you up on your kind offer," Jason replied.

As the two left the office, Colonel Ashby turned and yelled to Sergeant Emory, "Sergeant! Me and Jason are headed on over to Ellie's place if you need me."

The sergeant yelled back from the other room, "All right, Colonel. I'll watch the place."

At Miss Ellie's, Jason enjoyed the best meal he had eaten in a long time. Miss Ellie had a nice establishment. She ran the place all by herself, including doing all the cooking and baking. She had an upstairs living quarters with a few comfortable rooms fixed up nice for herself.

"You're right, Colonel," Jason said. "Miss Ellie does make the best biscuits a man could ever eat."

"Where you headed now, Jason? Not Ike's place, I hope?" the colonel asked.

"No, sir, Colonel," Jason said. "I don't have much of a hankerin' for whiskey tonight. I think I'll get some early shut-eye. In the mornin' I'll pick up some supplies, and I'll be headed back to my place. Winter's in the air, and I got to think about gettin' back to trappin'.

"You're welcome to bed down in the bunkhouse if you want, Jason," the colonel offered.

"Mighty kind of you, Colonel. That'll do just fine."

The next morning, Jason woke to the sound of a bugle playing revelry. *Well, that's a heck of a way to wake up out of a fine sleep*, Jason thought.

He walked over to the washbowl and splashed some cold water on his face. He glanced up and caught a look at himself in the mirror and almost didn't recognize the man looking back at him. His reflection really showed how weary he was feeling after his ordeal with Tikah and after being out on the trail for so long. He eyed his scraggly beard in the mirror and decided it was time to shave it off.

Jason got dressed, made a list of goods that would get him through the winter, and headed over to the general store. The large metal door squeaked as he opened it, and the wooden floors creaked as Jason walked toward the counter.

A voice from behind the counter asked, "What can I get for you, mister?"

Jason pulled out his list and said, "Plenty of each—coffee, flour, sugar, honey, grits, beans, and ammunition. That should take care of it." He would have ample meat once he got home and did some hunting between trapping.

The man said, "Comin' right up, mister. Hey, ain't you the guy who busted up Ike's place a while back?"

Jason replied, "Yep! That was me. The name's

McIvers, Jason McIvers. Mighty big shame that ole Ike got killed. No one in that brawl meant for that to happen."

"Yes, sir," the man said as he handed Jason a box filled with his supplies. "That'll be five dollars, Mr. McIvers."

Jason reached into his pocket and pulled out five silver dollars. "Much obliged," Jason said. He picked up the box and walked out the door. He crossed the street and went to the stable, where he paid the fifty-cent charge for his horse's board and walked the horse out into the open. As he loaded his supplies into his saddlebags, he heard a voice behind him.

"You wasn't gonna leave without sayin' goodbye?" the colonel asked.

"No, sir, Colonel. Just loadin' up first. I want to thank you again for the fine meal last night and a place to bed down," Jason said.

"Sure thing," the colonel said. "Guess we won't be seeing you for quite some time with trappin' season comin' up."

"No, sir," Jason said.

"Safe trip home. Be careful out there," the colonel said.

Jason mounted his horse. He turned toward the colonel, took a hold of the brim of his hat, and gave the colonel a nod. "I'll be headed out now."

The soldier in the guard tower yelled down, "Open the gate!" and Jason rode out.

The sun was shining, but the breeze was cold. Jason lifted his collar up tight around his neck. He tried hard not to think of Tikah during his long ride home, but he could not get her out of his mind. He wondered how long it would take Clayton and Tikah to get back to their tribe. He wondered if she would be welcomed back into the tribe. He wondered …

"Damn it!" he said out loud. "I gotta quit thinking about her." Jason spurred his horse and broke into a gallop. It would be a long day's ride, but Jason was anxious to get home. He had grown weary of sleeping on the ground.

Just as nightfall was upon him, Jason saw the silhouette of his cabin in the trees. He was home. The place sure looked good to him. Jason got off his horse and walked over to the shed. After lighting the lantern hanging at the door, he walked his horse to the stall. He removed the saddlebags and saddle and then put down a pile of hay and filled the water trough. He picked up the brush from the shelf and began brushing off the dust and sweat from his horse after the long journey.

Once Jason had finished tending to his horse, he picked up his saddlebags, took the lantern down from its hook, and walked across the yard to the cabin. He opened the door, flung the saddlebags onto the table, and sat down. He felt tired and isolated.

Come mornin', he thought, *I'll start workin' on gettin' those traps ready to set. Time to get back to work.*

Jason carried the lantern over to his bed. He pulled off his boots, got out of his dirty clothes, and lay on his bed. He leaned over and blew out the lantern.

CHAPTER **10**

It was morning. Jason woke to the sound of the wind blowing through the trees. The sun shined bright through the windows of his large one-room cabin. The cabin was cold, so Jason was forced to get out of his warm bed to start the fire. He put his britches on and walked over to the hearth. He still had some wood piled next to the hearth, so there was no need to go out in the cold just yet. He put the pot on the fire to make himself some coffee.

It's nice to be home, he thought as he reached down to pull his boots on. *Got a lot to get done around here before the first snowfall, startin' with gatherin' up and sortin' my traps.*

The smell of coffee quickly filled the cabin, and Jason poured his first cup. He sat at the table and eyed his surroundings. Jason had built the cabin a while back. It was a nice place for him to get out of the weather during the cold winter months. He enjoyed having the luxury of a roof over his head, comfortable furniture, a nice fire to keep him warm, and a place to cook his meals.

He thought about where he would set his traps this year as he sipped the hot coffee. He also thought about going hunting to get himself a nice-size buck. One good-size buck would be plenty of meat to last Jason pretty much all winter. And with the supplies he'd brought back from the fort, he was going to be eating well. The deer hide would bring a nice bounty too.

Maybe I'll set a few traps over on the hill south of here, he thought. He remembered seeing some tracks out that way. *And I might set a trap or two west of that, where I saw them mountain lion tracks. Those furs would bring a lot of money. On my way to the river, I'll set some smaller traps for martins, mink, and fox.*

Jason got up, poured himself another cup of coffee, and sat back down at the table. He thought, *I might even set a few more traps than last year in the river and catch me a few more beaver.* Beaver pelts made warm winter mittens and hats. There was a big demand for those around these parts in the winter. The smaller pelts were used for lining and fur collars. At the trading post Jason had been told that the folks back east had a real fancy for the mink and fox. The ladies liked them for their collars and hand muffs. *The women out west have a more practical use for them than just good looks*, he thought.

Hard as Jason tried to forget her by carrying on a conversation with himself in his mind, his thoughts wandered back to Tikah. As the wind blew outside, he wondered in the quiet of his cabin how she was getting along. Was she happy? Was she warm? *Well, it ain't any of my concern anymore. She's with Clayton. I gotta get to work.*

Jason put on his coat and hat and headed outside

to greet the day. The wind chilled his body before he buttoned up his coat and raised the collar tight around his neck. He headed out toward the shed, which doubled as a place to put his horse and a place to process his hides. *Someday I'm gonna build me a proper barn before this ole shed falls down*, he thought.

Jason went inside the shed and got his horse. He led him into the corral for some fresh air and a little exercise. Returning to the shed, Jason fumbled through all his traps and started hauling them out. He sorted them into piles by size and type of animal he hoped to catch. He took out his can of animal grease and rubbed some over each trap to protect the metal from rusting or freezing up. He assessed the condition of all his traps. Some of them needed a little work, but most remained in fine working shape and were ready to be set.

Jason had never had bad luck in these parts. Every year yielded him a good bounty, and no one had ever bothered his traps. He was the only trapper around for at least two hundred miles, best he knew. *Not many people crazy enough to try to make a living this far north, not in these brutal winters*, Jason thought. *Think I'll rest up today and then head out tomorrow and see if I can get me a buck.*

Jason spent the rest of the day splitting and stacking firewood. Nightfall came quickly. *The days are short this time of year*, Jason thought. He went to the corral and led his horse back into the shed for the night. He threw a pile of hay in front of the stall and put water in the trough. He closed the shed door, walked over to the cabin, and went inside.

At first light Jason headed out with his rifle to find

himself a buck. He hadn't been out more than an hour when he spotted a fine one off in the distance. Jason quietly climbed off his horse and got down on one knee to steady his aim. He waited for the perfect time and took the perfect shot. And just that quick, he had gotten himself plenty of meat to last all winter.

Jason ate well that night. He sat by the hearth after supper and felt grateful for his surroundings and what he had accomplished so far out in the middle of nowhere. *This is everything any normal human bein' could want*, he thought. *Well, almost everything.* Jason sighed and went to bed.

Morning came around quick and revealed a few inches of snow on the ground. Everything was covered under a blanket of white. There was a certain quietness that came when it snowed. Jason gathered up some of his traps and headed out. The weather was right for trapping. He would be a busy man for the next six months.

Fresh snow on the ground showed Jason just where to set his traps. He was an expert at telling what animals were in an area and where they were headed. Jason decided to set some traps in the river for beavers. He went to a few places where he had been lucky before and set more traps. Then he tried a couple of new spots. He was careful not to over trap in one area. *You want to keep the species surviving and reproducing for future winters*, he always told himself.

While searching for another new spot, he noticed some strange-looking tracks in the snow—they were not animal tracks but human tracks. And they were not the tracks of a white man's boots. Slowly, trying not to make a sound, Jason slipped his rifle out of its saddle holster.

It was loaded and ready to fire. Jason thought, *Wonder if this could be a brave from the Hokawa tribe that I heard about at the fort.*

The tracks were not deep, which told Jason that it was not a big man. Jason looked around for more sets of tracks, but he saw only the one set. Nightfall was closing in fast, and Jason didn't want to be in the woods come nightfall, especially with strange tracks around. He decided to head home and watch for more tracks in a few days when he came back to check his traps.

Jason was now on high alert. In the coming days, he kept a sharp eye and ear whenever he ventured away from the cabin. There was no telling who was out there. Jason remembered hearing a story from an Indian tracker at the fort about how Indians went off into the woods if they knew they were dying. It was their custom to ride out far away to a desolate place to be closer to the spirits of their ancestors who died before them. They knew they were dying when they saw the star of death. Maybe the tracks he had seen were from a dying Indian. Jason also remembered hearing about conflicts between Indian tribes just before he left the fort. *The tracks I saw out there might be related to that too*, Jason thought.

On the morning of the third day after he set his traps, Jason headed back out to where he had set traps near the river. The ground was white, with a foot of snow piled on the trail along the way. Jason found an animal in each of his traps. *These pelts should bring me a lot of money.* Each time he came to a trap, he released the frozen animal from its jaws, put the animal in a large pouch that hung from his saddle, and then reset the trap before moving on to the next one.

Jason continued along the path toward the river to check on his beaver traps. He wondered if he would spot more tracks by the river where he had seen them before. When he arrived, there were no tracks at all. Fresh snow had fallen and covered up any sign of tracks, all tracks, animal or otherwise.

When he reached the river, he went to his first trap and pulled it out. "This is a mighty big beaver! He ought to fetch me a fine bounty," Jason said as he lifted the beaver out of the ice-cold water. "Must be pretty near forty pounds, I'd say."

Jason reset the trap and moved on to where he set the next trap, about a quarter mile down the riverbed. Sure enough, Jason had himself another good-sized beaver. He pulled the dead beaver from the river and released it from the trap. He reset the trap and moved on.

Jason was excited about his luck with his traps, but he still thought about the human tracks he had seen the last time he was out there. He had not seen any new tracks at all but still thought it was strange and a little eerie. The thought that he was not alone in the woods was a little unnerving.

Jason had about all the animals he could carry and decided it was a good time to head back to the cabin. It was starting to snow, and that would make for a tough ride back. "Come on, boy," he said as he spurred his horse. "Let's go home."

Jason made good time riding home. By the time he reached the cabin, the snow had begun to fall much harder. He was glad to be home and decided he would stay home the next day and tend to his hides before heading back out. *Hopefully, by then the snow will have eased up a bit,* Jason thought as he unloaded the animals and put them in the shed along with his horse.

He went inside the cabin and was able to start the fire easily enough from the coals still smoldering from the morning. He took off his wet coat and hat and hung them by the fire. He threw a potato on the hot coals and heated himself some deer meat.

While Jason's potato cooked and his meat warmed, he sat at the table and thought about where he would set his traps next. He jot down a list of places that have been profitable for him in the past. They were difficult locations but they always paid off. After about an hour when his potato was cooked and his meat was heated, Jason cleared a spot at the table. He brought a plate of food over, sat down and began to eat. Once he was full, Jason pushed himself away from the table. *It's been a good day*, he thought. *Think I'll get some shut-eye.* He pulled off his boots, took off his clothes, and went to bed. It did not take long for him to fall asleep.

In the morning Jason fixed himself some grits and a pot of coffee before going out to the shed to work on his furs. It had stopped snowing, and the wind was calm, but it was bitter cold outside. Jason spent the whole day in the shed and managed to skin every animal and process every skin.

Tomorrow I'll hit the trail again and check on the traps, Jason thought. He blew out the lantern, closed the door to the shed, and went in the cabin.

CHAPTER 11

J ason was up before sunrise and decided to head out as soon as the sun came up. He ate a good breakfast before going outside to saddle up his horse. He brought the horse around and tied him up near the corral and then went back in the cabin to get a box of rifle shells, a wool blanket, jerky, and water to bring along. He put his coat on, grabbed his hat, and walked out the door. As Jason was about to mount his horse, he noticed smoke far off in the distance. He wasn't real sure what he was seeing at first, but then he thought it could be smoke from a campfire. It seemed like an awful lot of smoke for a campfire, though.

Well, that makes no sense, he thought. *There's no one around these parts within two hundred miles. But with that much smoke, does someone want to be found? Maybe it's that Hokawa Indian that was roamin' around out there by the river ... No, can't be. If it was an Indian up in the hills to die, he wouldn't be lightin' no fire. Well, I can't worry about it now. Time to get movin'.* He spurred his horse and rode off for another day.

On this day Jason decided to ride south and set his traps in areas that had been profitable for him in years past. The smoke he had seen was north of his place, so he did not think of it for the rest of the day. By the time he headed back to the cabin, the sun was low in the sky, and the smoke was no longer visible. Jason didn't give it another thought.

The rest of his night was like all others. After finishing all the chores around the place, Jason sat near the hearth and stared into the fire. The flames were mesmerizing. They had a calming effect on Jason, and soon his mind wandered to the smoke he had seen earlier that day. *Think I'll ride north tomorrow and see what I can find out about that smoke. Mighty strange*, Jason thought. His eyes felt heavy. "Guess I'll get some shut-eye," he said aloud. Jason went to bed and fell right to sleep.

Early the next morning, Jason saddled his horse for the day's ride. He slung a large pouch over the animal. He was confident that he would fill it that day. It was bitter cold outside, but the sky was clear, and although more snow had fallen during the night, it had stopped now. Jason mounted his horse and looked north in the direction where he had seen the smoke the day before, but there was no sign of it now. *Mighty strange*, he thought again as he spurred his horse and trotted off.

Jason's bounty continued to grow as he checked his traps along the way. It was a cold, hard, lonely way of life, but it was the only life Jason knew. He thought about what he would spend his money on when he went to the fort to sell his pelts. It had been a long time since Jason had had a drink; there had been none since the incident at Ike's place. That tragic event had left its mark on Jason, and though he knew he had not literally killed Ike, the colonel was right—had the ruckus Jason started not happened, Ike would be alive today.

Jason eyed the ground as he rode the trail from trap to trap. The snow was deeper than the last time he had ridden through this area, but there were no fresh tracks of any kind. Still, he knew there would be something in the next trap he rode up on. And sure enough, he was right. He came upon a real nice fox. "Got one," he said out loud. "This is a mighty fine-lookin' fox. Nice and big with fine color. This fur will bring some good money."

Jason got off his horse and released the frozen fox from the trap. Then he reset the trap and put more bait on it. He carefully placed it back on the ground and covered it with snow. It was his normal routine to completely camouflage the traps. Jason put the fox in his pouch before mounting his horse. He thought that he would ride a little further and check one more trap on the way to the river. He then would check those river traps before circling back toward the cabin.

The next trap Jason came upon had been triggered, but there was nothing caught in it. Jason could see blood around the trap and said to himself, "It happens. Sometimes critters get caught in the trap and somehow manage to get free." Jason reset the trap with fresh bait. He looked around for tracks, but the fresh snow covered any sign of what had wandered too close to his trap.

Jason continued on his route. He could hear the sound of the river flowing as he neared it. He thought about fishing a little. He said to himself, "Addin' some fish to my meat stockpile would be a tasty change from venison once in a while." But the day was growing shorter, and Jason thought it might be better to check the last trap and head on back to the cabin. *I'll fish next time*, he thought. Thinking about fish reminded him of the fish Tikah had fixed for him while he recovered from his wounds. *Sure wish I knew what she did to make that fish taste so dang good.*

The last trap in the river was empty. He checked its setting and saw that it was still ready to bite down on the next beaver that came too close. Jason knew that next time there would be something there for him. He got back on his horse, turned south, and headed for home.

He had not gone far when he heard an unfamiliar sound nearby. He was curious and on high alert. *What is that?* he asked himself. *Doesn't sound like any animal, wounded or otherwise, that I'm familiar with.* He decided to head in the direction of the sound and see if he could find the source. *It could be that critter that got away from my trap. Hate the thought of any animal sufferin'*, Jason thought.

He rode a little further before he came upon a sight that he couldn't quite make out. He pulled his rifle out of its holster as he rode a little closer. The sound grew louder as he approached. To Jason's shock and disbelief, he finally saw that it was Tikah!

"Tikah!" he shouted. "My God, Tikah!"

She was unconscious and near death. Jason holstered his rifle and jumped off his horse. He ran over to her, falling along the way in the deep snow. When he reached Tikah, he could feel that she was cold. At first she did not respond to him.

He shook her and wrapped his arms around her and kept saying her name. "Tikah! Tikah, can you hear me? Tikah, open your eyes. Can you hear me?"

He ran back to his horse and grabbed the wool blanket that he always carried with him whenever he ventured away from the cabin in the winter. He wrapped Tikah in the blanket to try to warm her up. While wrapping the blanket around her, he noticed that her foot was badly injured. In horror, he thought, *The trap! The trap that went off and had blood around it—Tikah must have stepped on the trap!*

He continued to rock Tikah, and she opened her eyes. When she realized that she was in Jason's arms, she tried to speak, but all she could do was smile. A huge sense of relief came over her. She knew she would be safe. Her journey alone was over.

"Tikah, thank God you are alive. Hang on. Hang on, Tikah." Jason's thoughts raced from one question to another. *Why is she here? How did she get here? Where is Clayton?* Then he thought about the smoke he had seen in the distance. *The smoke I saw yesterday must have been Tikah. It was a signal fire.*

Jason tried to decide what he should do. Should he make camp here for the night and start out with Tikah in the morning? Or should they head out for the cabin right away? *She's hurt bad*, Jason thought. *Best if we just leave now. No tellin' how much more snow will fall tonight, and it's too cold for her out here.*

Jason picked up Tikah and put her on his horse in front of the saddle. Then he got on. With one arm around

Tikah and the other holding the reins, he spurred his horse, and they left.

It was nightfall before they reached the cabin. The trip had been long. With deeper snow on the ground, it took longer to travel. Jason rode up to the cabin and dismounted. He reached for Tikah and gently pulled her off the horse. She was cold and barley responsive. He carried her into the cabin, laid her on his bed, and lit the lantern. Jason quickly started a fire to warm the place up and then went back outside to put his horse in the shed.

When he got back into the cabin, he thought, *I got to get her out of those wet clothes.* He sat her up and began to remove her clothing. How well Jason remembered Tikah's small, dark-skinned body and her beautiful long black hair. She had a young body that had not begun to show signs of age. He gently laid her back down on his bed and propped her head up on a pillow. He reached for a dry, warm blanket. As Jason pulled the blanket over Tikah, he noticed her belly—just slightly swollen. *She's with child*, he thought. He quickly covered her with the blanket and walked over to the hearth to throw more wood on the fire.

Jason was beginning to fix Tikah something to eat when he heard her voice.

"Jason. Jason, I found you."

He stopped what he was doing and rushed over to her. "Tikah, rest. Try not to talk right now. You're safe; I will take care of you."

"Jason, I have come far to find you. I—"

"Not now, Tikah. Rest." As he pulled the blanket

snugly up around her neck, Tikah closed her eyes, and with a smile on her face, she fell asleep.

While Tikah's food was warming over the fire, Jason thought it best to tend to her foot. It was wrapped, but the bandages were dirty and wet. They had to come off. Jason lifted the blanket from her foot. He got a pot of warm water and began to clean her foot the best he could.

Tikah moaned a bit and woke up as Jason put some healing ointment on the wound. He was glad that he had brought the ointment back from the fort a while back. "Sorry, Tikah, but this has to be cleaned up. Your foot is bad hurt. How did this happen?"

"You are a good trapper, Jason," Tikah said. "You hide your traps well. I was coming to you. I knew this must be the area where you trap, from what you told me on our journey. I thought all I had to do was find a trap, and you would find me—only I did not plan to step on one. It was hidden well in the snow, and I did not see it. I was on my way to the river to get some water.

"The teeth of your traps are very sharp. My moccasins were no match. The trap grabbed my foot, and at first I could not free myself. The grip was strong, but I kept pulling on the trap until I was finally able to open it and free my foot. I knew it was bad, and I wrapped it the best I could. It bled a lot. I had strength only to build a fire, a large fire, and try to keep warm. I hoped you would see the smoke. But the fire burned out, and strength left my body."

Jason caressed her face and said, "Rest. We'll talk more after you have had something to eat."

Tikah felt overwhelmed with joy. She had found Jason, and she knew everything would work out just as they had planned when they were on their journey to the Cave of the Great Ones.

Jason's mind was racing. He didn't know what to make of any of this. Tikah was with child. But where was Clayton? Did Clayton know that she was carrying Clayton's child? He had so many questions.

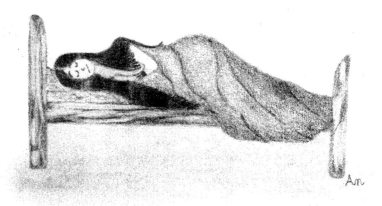

CHAPTER 12

The food warming in the pot was ready. Jason removed a bowl from the cupboard and quickly inspected it to be sure it was clean. He did the same for the spoon he took out of the drawer. He picked up a clean cloth from the table as he walked back over to the fire. Jason set the bowl on the hearth while he lifted the hot pot from the fire using a hook he had made. Jason spooned a small amount of broth and meat into the bowl and hoped that Tikah would like the taste. He walked over to the bed and noticed that Tikah was watching him with a smile on her face.

"Oh, you're awake," he said, pulling up a chair to sit next to the bed. "I fixed you a little something to eat. I hope you like it."

Tikah sat up and leaned back against the large wooden headboard that Jason had made himself. He liked working with wood and making furniture in the warmer months of the year when he wasn't trapping.

Cheaper than buying furniture, and mine is made a lot better! he would always say to himself when he finished a piece.

Jason gently placed the cloth over Tikah's chest and began to spoon-feed her. "Probably not as good as your cookin'," he said, "but it will fill your stomach and make you strong again."

"It is fine, Jason. It tastes good," Tikah said. After eating about half of what Jason had spooned in the bowl, Tikah said, "Jason, I have much to tell you."

"I have so many questions I want to ask," Jason said.

"Please, let me talk," said Tikah. "All your questions will be answered when you hear my words."

Jason put the spoon back in the bowl and gently took the cloth from Tikah's chest. He stood, walked over to the hearth, put what remained in the bowl back in the pot, and covered it. He then walked back over to Tikah, sat down on the chair, and said, "Go on, Tikah. Tell me what you have to say." Jason was nervous and afraid of what he was about to hear, but it had to be said.

"Jason," Tikah said, "at first when Pale One found me in the cave, I was very happy. I had thought I was going to die in the Cave of the Great Ones. It would have been all right if I did die, for my prayer was answered, and my father is now riding with the Great Ones for all eternity. I asked Pale One how he found me, and he said that some of the people from our tribe had told him of the cave and described where it was. They also told him that no living soul had ever been there. Pale One said that a man rode along with him and knew of the cave, but he never spoke your name. Was that man you, Jason?" she asked.

"Yes, Tikah, it was me," he answered.

"He also did not say how he met this man. Can you now tell me how you and Pale One met?"

"I met Clayton at Fort Ryerson," Jason said. "I had been at the fort longer than I wanted to be. I was hurt in the explosion at the cave after the gunfight broke out between Straton, Travis, and the army soldiers, when you were hiding in the tunnel. The colonel had tracked down Straton and his men after Straton and me didn't show up at Fort Cross to deliver a package to the colonel's daughter. It was her dowry, money he saved to give to his daughter on her wedding day. Straton had planned all along to steal the dowry, kill me, and make it look like Indians did it. After the explosion I was hurt bad. I fell from the ledge onto the ground. Colonel Ashby's men took me back to the fort so the colonel's personal medic could tend to me. The whole time I was at the fort, all I could think of was you. The colonel said I even called out your name a few times when I was still unconscious."

Jason got up and put another piece of wood in the fire, then came back and sat down next to Tikah. "Anyways," he continued, "the time came when I was better, and I was ready to leave the fort when Clayton rode in. He got off his horse and tied it up near where I was sitting. He told me his name, and I told him mine. I asked him where he was headed, and he told me the story of the Cave of the Great Ones. While talking he said your name, and right away I knew I had to go with him to find out what had happened to you after the explosion. I did not tell Clayton that I knew you because from what Clayton said, I got the idea you were his. As much as those words stung, I still had to find out if you were alive. During the three days and two nights we spent on the trail, I never told him about us. How could I? You were not mine to have."

"So that is why you were not there when Pale One found me," Tikah said, "and that is why he did not think it was important to say your name. It was because he did not know about us."

"Yes," Jason said. "Once I knew you were alive and Clayton would take care of you, I decided to leave. I climbed back down the mountain. I watered Clayton's horse and rode out." Jason stared at the flames in the fireplace the whole time he spoke. He could not make himself look at Tikah. "Ain't no man wants to hear that his woman was with another man. I could not let myself come between you and the man you loved."

Tikah said, "It is my time to speak, Jason. First, my heart has ached for you since I last saw you. I too wondered if you were alive or dead. I dared not speak your name to Pale One until I had a chance to tell him my story when we got back to our people.

"Yes, I loved Pale One, but not as you think. I loved Pale One as a brother. We were as close as two people could be, but not in the way you think. Pale One always hoped that someday I would become his wife, but I never had those feelings for him. And even though he was accepted into our tribe, he was a white man. It is forbidden for any Opoka to marry one who is not of our kind. Pale One had hoped that one day my father would make an exception and allow a union between us. Then, as you know, my father was killed in a battle against the

Hokawas, so Pale One never got the permission he had hoped for, and I never had to tell him I did not love him in that way."

Jason interrupted. "You 'loved' Pale One? 'Were' close? 'Was' a white man? What are you saying, Tikah?"

"Let me finish, Jason," she said. "One day we got word of another uprising coming our way. Pale One thought that surely the elders of the tribe would allow a union between us if he rode out in battle with the warriors of our tribe. The elders allowed him to ride, even though my father had never allowed it. But Pale One was not a warrior—he knew not the ways of fighting—and early on in the battle, Pale One was killed."

Jason was stunned and could not find the right words to comfort Tikah.

She continued, "I was heartbroken to hear that Pale One had been killed. The Opokas were strong in that battle, and we lost only three braves. It was a sad day when their spirits were set free during the ceremony of the dead. But there was one thing that I was happy about, and that was that Pale One never found out about my love for you. He joined the great spirits above, leaving behind the one he loved and hoped to marry someday without ever knowing the truth. Once the ceremony was over, I did not know what I would do with myself. My heart ached for you, and I felt great sorrow for Pale One. I also knew something else."

Tikah paused for a moment. She took hold of Jason's hand. She lowered the blanket, exposing her naked body, and put Jason's hand on her belly. "I am with child, Jason. Your child. You are the only man that I have given my body and soul to. But my people will never accept our love and the child I now carry. So that is why I left without telling them, and that is why I had to find you."

Jason gently put both of his hands on Tikah's belly. He leaned over and kissed her belly and then kissed her lips. "You are home, Tikah. You are mine, and I will spend the rest of my life with you. We will raise a fine baby and maybe have another someday. We have a lifetime together ahead of us, and no one can ever take that away from us."

Jason got up, walked over to the fire, and added another piece of wood. He then sat back down beside Tikah. He pulled off his boots, took off his clothes, and blew out the lantern. Darkness filled the room except for the glow from the fire. Jason got into bed beside Tikah and held her warm body close to his. No more words were spoken. The fire and passion they felt for each other while on the trail to the Cave of the Great Ones ignited once again. Tikah and Jason resumed their love and devotion to each other and made love that night.

Jason awoke to a beautiful morning. He got out of bed, slipped on his britches, and put a piece of wood on the fire. Jason got his coffee pot ready to make coffee, just as he did every morning. But this morning was different. He had a feeling of peace and calm about him. He glanced over at Tikah; she was still sleeping peacefully under the warm blanket. Jason walked over to the window and saw a thick blanket of new snow on the ground. The air was quiet all around. Normally, Jason would put on his warmest clothes, grab his winter coat and hat, and ride out to tend his traps. But Jason had other plans today. He would stay in the cabin and spend the day tending to Tikah's wounded foot instead.

Jason quietly finished dressing and splashed some water on his face. He grabbed his winter coat and hat off the coatrack and went outside to feed the horse and gather a few more pieces of firewood. When he came back into the cabin, Tikah was awake and sitting up in bed.

She smiled and said, "The white man's bed is very nice. Much nicer than our furs on the dirt floor of our lodge."

"I'm glad you approve," Jason said. "There are a lot of ways that are different between your people and mine. But we will learn each other's customs and soon make new ones of our own. How does your foot feel?"

"It is much better. I think I would like to try to walk a little," she said.

Jason went to the dresser drawer and pulled out a clean white nightshirt. He handed it to Tikah and said, "It ain't pretty, but it will do until we can get your clothes cleaned up."

She smiled and took the nightshirt. After slipping it over her head, she stood up, putting most of her weight on her good foot, and allowed the nightshirt to gently float over the rest of her body.

Jason then helped her over to the table and chair near the fire. "We got a lot of plannin' to do, Tikah," he said. "I got to build a cradle for our little one before he gets here."

"He!" Tikah exclaimed.

"Well, I can't say for sure, but I got a gut feelin', and my gut feelins are usually right," Jason said. "And I gotta build you a fine rockin' chair to set by the fire so you can rock our little one to sleep."

Tikah smiled and felt truly loved. She said to Jason, "We will have to hunt a deer so I can cure and tan the hide to make myself another dress. The one I have now will not fit around the middle much longer. And I could use another pair of moccasins to wear indoors."

Jason walked over to Tikah and put his hand on her belly. "I got somethin' out in the shed that might work. But that can wait. Let's take a look at those bandages before you make any more plans that involve you gettin' up and moving around." He unwrapped the bandage and looked at Tikah's foot. The swelling had gone down some, and it was healing well. He put more ointment on the wound and bandaged it up with clean strips of cloth.

"Come tomorrow mornin', I'm going to have to ride out and tend to my traps. Can't leave them to fend for themselves for too long," Jason said. "But for today, I'm going to stay home and tend to some chores around the place."

"When my foot is better," Tikah said, "I too will help with chores around here. I can cook for you, and I can clean, and I can also cure and tan hides. Opoka women are very good at tending to hides. We are also very good at putting a woman's soft touch where we live."

Jason smiled and said, "Sounds mighty fine, Tikah. Sounds like we're gonna make a fine team."

CHAPTER 13

The pair spent the rest of their day in the cabin. Jason tended to Tikah, and they sat at the table and talked most of the day away, telling each other about their days since Jason left Tikah with Clayton at the cave. The day remained clear with no new snowfall.

At nightfall Jason lit the lanterns. He hoped that come morning, it would be a good day to ride out and tend to his traps. He asked Tikah to stay in the cabin the next day while he was gone. Her foot needed to get better before she wandered outside. Stubbornly, she agreed. Tikah was not one to sit around all day and do nothing. It was not the way of the Opoka women. There were many chores for women to do, and doing nothing did not sit well with her.

Jason put a piece of wood in the fire. After dinner Jason and Tikah sat in their chairs near the hearth. It was good to be warm. The flames were mesmerizing, and few words were spoken until Jason said, "I think we better get some shut-eye. I got an early mornin' comin'."

Jason helped Tikah from her chair to the bed, where she sat and waited for Jason to put one more piece of wood in the fire and blow out the lantern. Jason took off his boots and clothes and sat down next to Tikah. With the glow from the fire dimly lighting the room, Jason put his hand on Tikah's belly and said, "Get some rest, little one. There's a big world out here waitin' for you."

Tikah smiled and lay down in bed. Jason climbed in beside her and pulled the covers over both of them. Sleep came quick as they lay together in each other's arms.

Jason was up at daybreak. The sky was clear, and the sun was shining. He had a long day ahead of him, and the sooner he got started, the sooner he would get back to the cabin. Before he left, he retrieved the buckskin that had been drying and stretching on the rack and hung it out in the sunshine. He would bring it in for Tikah when he got back home.

Tikah also got up early. Jason again asked her to stay inside and reminded her that she would have plenty to do once her foot healed. She agreed and waved from the door as Jason rode off.

It was a good day to be out riding. The sun was shining, and the wind was calm. There was about two feet of snow on the ground, but it wasn't as cold as it had been. Jason thought, *Tomorrow I need to get workin' on those hides I brought home a while back. Gonna take me a day or two to get caught up on them before I ride out again.*

Tikah was able to get around pretty well. After Jason left, she got dressed and cleaned up a little around the cabin. She noticed how quiet it was outside. She grew weary from boredom and decided to go outside for a while and let the sun shine on her. She brought a chair out on the porch. It was cold, but the sun felt good. Her eyes wandered over to the corral and then to the shed. She thought, *That must be where Jason works on his hides.*

Before she knew it, she was up and walking toward the shed. She opened the door, and the light shined bright into the space inside. She could see many pelts in all different stages of processing. She thought, *I will be a great help for Jason. Opoka women are good at tanning hides. There is much to do here.* She looked around a little more and saw the buckskin outside in the sun. Her eyes lit up, and she thought, *That will be my new dress. I can even make a new pair of moccasins from the same hide. And there is enough fur here for me to use just a little to line the inside of my winter moccasins.* Delighted, she said out loud, "There are many hides here. I don't think Jason will mind if, just this once, I use a little for myself."

She walked over to the buckskin, felt its softness, and said, "This is ready." Tikah cut the hide from its tethers. She rolled it up, put it under her arm, and slowly made her way back to the cabin. She looked around for tools that she could use to cut and sew the pieces of her new dress. Tikah found a sharp knife and sinew that Jason had harvested from the deer. When Tikah was a young girl, her mother had taught her that sinew made good twine and thread. She also crafted a needle from a bone fragment she had found in the shed. Tikah held the pieces of buckskin up to herself to make sure she left plenty of room for her belly to grow, and then she began hand-stitching what would become her new dress.

The day passed quickly. The sun was low in the sky.

Tikah had prepared supper in the pot and was keeping it warm on the hearth. Jason would be home soon, and she wanted to please him with a surprise. The cabin was warm from the fire.

Jason was on his way back to the cabin with another full pouch of furs. His traps had proven to be well placed. He could see the cabin off in the distance, and he stopped for a minute to take in the beauty of what he saw. There was a warm glow of light shining through the windows, and he could see smoke coming out of the chimney. *Ain't that a pretty sight?* he thought. *Sure beats comin' home to a dark, cold cabin.*

Jason spurred his horse and slowly trotted the remaining way in the deep snow. His excitement grew as he got closer to the cabin. When he arrived, he walked his horse into the shed and tied him up for the night. He did not see the buckskin outside where he had left it and began to wonder. He unloaded his still-frozen animals and said to himself, "I'll tend to this tomorrow. Right now I wanna get inside and see Tikah."

Jason went up on the porch and stomped the snow off his boots. He opened the door and saw Tikah standing inside with her hands behind her back. She was wearing a new dress and moccasins, and she had a big smile on her face. He could see her growing belly pressing against the buckskin.

"Ain't you a sight for sore eyes?" Jason said as he walked inside and closed the door.

"You like it, Jason?" she asked.

Jason walked over to Tikah and put his hand on her belly. "Mighty fine."

"You are not upset with me for using your buckskin for my new clothes?" she asked.

Jason responded, "Ain't no better use for that hide than what I see right here."

"Come, sit down," Tikah said. "I have a hot meal ready for you."

Jason looked over at the table and saw that Tikah had set it with plates and forks from the cupboard and drawer.

Tikah noticed Jason looking at a small piece of greenery she'd picked from outside. She put it in a jar with water and placed it on the supper table for a centerpiece. "This is the best I can do for now. Winter snow covers all the flowers."

Jason walked over to the table and thought about how lucky he was. Then he said, "I am pleased, Tikah. You make me very happy. But what did I say about not going outside while I was gone?"

Tikah walked over to Jason and hugged him. She knew she could melt his heart with the mere press of her body pressed against his. "Please do not be angry," she said. "I grew weary from boredom. I was very careful."

"How could I be mad, Tikah? Yes, you have pleased me very much."

Tikah had prepared a nice meal with meat using spices she had brought in her pouch when she set out to find Jason. She had found flour in the flour bin and made something that Jason had never eaten before.

Jason eyed it and said, "What do you call it?"

"We call it flatbread," Tikah answered. "It is what we have with all our meals. Here, let me show you." Tikah took a few pieces of the tender meat and rolled them in the flatbread. She handed it to Jason and said, "Try it."

Jason bit into the flatbread and meat and said, "This is very good, Tikah. I like it."

"I will fix you many meals that my mother taught me to cook, and you will never go hungry. When the spring comes, I will be able to add more kinds of food to the table."

Jason told Tikah that he had always wanted to plant a garden but had been too busy to tend to it. Maybe now they would grow one together. Tikah was pleased. She was not a farmer, but she was willing to learn and care for Jason's garden.

"Until things grow," she told Jason, "I will search in the woods and find many roots, herbs, and berries once the snow has melted."

Jason said, "I'm a lucky man, Tikah."

She smiled and put her hands on her belly. "I will make you a good wife, Jason."

The night ended as they all did. As the days passed, the darkness became a special part of every day for Jason and Tikah. They both settled into life together, and they were each grateful for the other. One night turned into another, and the weeks soon turned into months.

Jason woke one morning at sunup. He rolled over to put his hand on Tikah's belly, but she was not lying beside him. Jason sat up in a panic and looked around the room until he saw Tikah sitting by the hearth, staring into the fire. She was wearing the dress she had made a few months ago, and it was now tight around the middle. Jason could see that she was gently caressing her large belly.

"Are you okay, Tikah?" Jason asked.

"Oh!" she said, startled out of her quiet thoughts. "Jason, you are awake."

Jason got out of bed and slipped on his britches. He walked over to Tikah, and she stood up to greet him. Jason reached for Tikah's large belly, as he had done several times every day and every night since Tikah came to him.

"The time is near, Jason," Tikah said. "This little one grows impatient of being inside me."

Jason could feel the movement inside Tikah's belly. "Yes," he said, "the time is near. I need to get to work on that cradle right away."

Tikah smiled and put her arms around Jason. They walked over to the table and sat down, and Tikah said, "First, you need nourishment, Jason McIvers. Then the cradle."

They enjoyed their first meal of the day together. Jason looked out the window and took note of the melting snow. Spring was coming, and his trapping was about over for another season. Soon he would need to ride out to the fort and sell his furs. But he would not leave the cabin this close to the time of Tikah giving birth.

After breakfast Jason put on his heavy coat and went out to the shed. The sun was shining, and the sky was blue, so he decided to put his horse in the corral.

Tikah stayed in the cabin. She sat near the hearth and thought, *I live well as the wife of a white man.* Her thoughts wandered to all the things she wanted to do after the baby was born. She was a good hide tanner, and Jason had a lot of hides that needed tending to. She thought about wandering outside every day to find something to eat with their meals. She also thought about the many plants that she would gather and have on hand for whatever sicknesses might come along. *My mother taught me well the value of certain plants for healing*, she thought.

The days were getting longer as the snowpack began to melt. Jason had spent most of the day in the shed, and Tikah began to worry about him. He had not even come in for something to eat. Just then, Tikah heard Jason's boots on the wooden porch. The door quickly opened, and Jason walked in carrying a beautiful cradle lined with soft fur.

Tikah's eyes lit up when she saw the cradle. "Is that what you have been working on all day in the shed?"

Jason replied, "Yes, Tikah. The time is near. Do you like it?"

The cradle Jason had made was very different from the cradleboards the women of her tribe put their babies on. This cradle was special. Tikah would be able to rock the cradle while their baby slept inside. With her hands on her swollen belly, she looked at Jason and said, "Yes, Jason. This will do. Our baby will sleep warm in this cradle."

She went to one of the drawers of the dresser. She pulled out a small swaddling cloth she had made from extra pieces of the buckskin hide she had used to make her dress and moccasins. "He will be very warm wrapped in this while lying in his cradle," she said.

"He!" Jason said. "He will be warm," he said with a smile on his face.

"Yes, Jason, I think our baby will be a fine, strong boy."

Jason put the cradle down near the hearth. He stood back and admired it one last time before they walked over to the table to eat supper.

After supper, Tikah said to Jason, "I am tired. I must go lie down. Our baby has taken my energy during these last few days. I need to rest a lot so I will be strong when he is born."

Jason helped Tikah remove her moccasins and take off her dress. Then he helped her get in bed. Jason admired her beautiful naked body and caressed her swollen belly before he pulled the blanket over her. He put a few more pieces of wood in the fire and then sat down and pulled off his boots. He took his clothes off, blew out the lantern, and got into bed beside Tikah.

Tikah said, "Soon our life will change. We are bringing a new one into the world, and we will have a lot to teach him."

Jason said, "He will be strong and smart. He will need little—I'll see to that. Someday when he is older, I will teach him how to hunt, trap, and cure hides."

Jason's hand once again found its way to Tikah's belly. He fell asleep while the baby moved under his hand.

CHAPTER 14

S pring arrived, bringing a new day and a new baby. Tikah and Jason's son was born in the early morning hours. He was a strong baby. His skin was not as dark as Tikah's, but his hair was as black as a raven's wing, just like his mother's. Jason was filled with pride. He thought about how far he had come from the drunken, unruly man he once had been back at the fort. Trapping was a lonely life, but Jason hadn't minded back then. He hadn't much liked being around people with all their proper and civilized ways. But he was very different now, different as night and day, and he liked where his new life had taken him. He knew it was all because of the love of this woman.

Breaking into Jason's thoughts, Tikah said, "Jason, I have been thinking of a name for our son. Hear me first, then tell me what you think."

Jason turned to Tikah and said, "Tell me, Tikah. I'm listenin'."

"I have been thinking of this for a long time now,"

she said, "and I thought if our baby was born a boy, I would like to name him Clayton. You know how I loved Pale One as my brother; we were always very close. But most of all, Jason, if it were not for Pale One, you and I never would have crossed paths again along our journey in life. I would like to remember him and honor him in this way." Tikah paused, took a deep breath, and said, "Now tell me what you think."

Without hesitation Jason said, "Clayton. Clayton McIvers. I like the sound of that, and I like your thought behind it. Yes, our son will be named Clayton."

Tikah smiled and reached for Jason's hand. "So it will be!"

Tikah was a strong woman, and it was not long before she was back up and moving around. She was anxious to begin doing all the things she could only think about during the last few months, when it was winter and she was with child.

In a few days Jason would ride to the fort and sell all his furs. He went to the shed and began to bundle up the large load and stack it in the buckboard. *These will bring a handsome amount of money*, he thought.

Jason would stock up on supplies from the general store before riding home the next day. He was anxious to see the colonel again and tell him of the arrival of his new son. Colonel Ashby saw the good in Jason in spite of Jason's wild ways. The colonel knew deep inside that he was a good man, and Jason had grown fond of the colonel. Jason had never held it against the colonel when he had Jason locked up after one of his many brawls at

Ike's place. Jason knew he had deserved it, even if he hadn't to take too kindly to it.

A couple of days later, Jason was ready to ride out bright and early. It was a long one-day ride to the fort, so an early start was in order. Jason hugged Tikah, kissed the top of Clayton's head, and said to Tikah, "Take good care of our boy."

Tikah smiled and said, "I will, Jason, and you take good care of yourself. I will see you late tomorrow."

Jason rode off in the buckboard. Tikah stood there holding Clayton in her arms and watched Jason until she could no longer see him. She turned and went into the cabin and closed the door behind her.

After a long ride, Jason finally arrived at the fort, where he heard the familiar words from the guard tower. "Rider comin'!"

Soon after, the gate opened, and Jason quickly rode in as the gate closed behind him. Jason was surprised to see the number of civilians within the walls of the fort. *Must be more settlers arriving*, he thought as he rode over to Colonel Ashby's office.

At the office, he jumped down from the buckboard, tied his horse up at the hitching post, and went inside the small building.

"Yes, sir, can I help you?" a soldier asked Jason. Jason was not familiar with this man's face.

Jason answered, "I am hopin' to see the colonel. Tell him it's McIvers."

"Wait right here, McIvers," said the soldier.

Jason turned to face the window and was in awe at the goings-on outside. The last time he was in the fort, it had been pretty much deserted. Just then the inner office door opened, and Jason heard the familiar voice of the colonel.

"Well, I'll be! If it ain't Jason McIvers! Come in, son. Come in and sit down." The colonel walked behind his desk and sat down.

Jason followed him and sat in the chair in front of the desk.

"Look at you, all cleaned up and looking healthy," the colonel said. "Ya here to sell your furs?"

Jason replied, "Yes, sir, I am. And I come to tell you some good news."

The colonel said, "We can always use some good news around these parts. What's your news?"

Jason paused for a minute and said, "Well, Colonel, I'm the father of a fine baby boy!"

The colonel's eyes lit up, and a big smile came over his face. He stood and walked over to Jason, gave him a solid handshake, and said, "Congratulations, son! A baby boy—well, I'll be! Who's the lucky lady? Last we talked, you said you was just chasin' the wind."

"Yes, sir, Colonel," said Jason, "but things took a turn for the better. I found her, Colonel. I found Tikah. We've been together ever since. And now we have a son together."

The colonel walked back over to his desk and sat down. There was a pause for a moment, and then he said, "Now you know, son, it makes no difference to me who you marry—that's your business. And I know how much you must care for this woman, seein' what you went through to find her and all. And I want to say how happy I am for you. But you gotta know, not all the folks comin' into these parts and formin' all these new settlements will be as happy about your news as I am, if you know what I mean."

Jason listened to the colonel's words and let them sink in. He noticed that the smile had left the colonel's face. "Well, Colonel, I reckon you mean because Tikah is an Opoka Indian, and that makes our son half-Indian and half-white. But Tikah ain't no different than the finest white woman there ever was. Tikah is every bit as good as they are and then some. I'll bet none of them fine white women can ride a horse, hunt, or prepare hides like Tikah can. And I'll bet not a one of them can love a man any more than she can. I'm mighty sorry to hear that some people may not be too keen on the idea, but that don't much matter to me, sir."

A smile came back on the colonel's face, and he said, "Does this new son of yours have a name?"

"It's Clayton. Clayton McIvers," Jason said proudly. "We named him after Tikah's brother."

"You mean Pale One?" the colonel asked. "Pale One is Tikah's brother?"

"Yes, sir. But he was killed in one of them Indian uprisings that have been happenin'. Clayton was not Tikah's brother by blood, but he was as much of a brother as one could ever be. When Clayton was a boy, five or six years old, Clayton's whole wagon train got wiped out durin' an Indian attack led by the Hokawa tribe. Tikah's father and his braves happened on the scene after the attack and found the boy alive. He was the only one who survived. He had been hiding under a blanket under the floorboards of a wagon. The chief had a big heart and could not leave the boy there to die. So he brought him back to Tikah's tribe and let him grow up among his people. Pale One and Tikah were very close for the rest of his life. And to honor him, we decided to name our firstborn Clayton."

"Well, that makes sense," said the colonel. "Ain't no better reason than that. Clayton McIvers! Well, I'll be!"

Jason and the colonel talked together for quite a while. Jason learned of the deluge of new settlers coming out west to start a new life. The fort had grown to accommodate them, with new shops and businesses having opened to sell goods and provide services to the many people arriving.

"What has everyone so fired up about comin' west, Colonel?" Jason asked.

The colonel said, "Gold, gold fever. Everyone's hopin' to be that next one to strike it rich. City folk don't have enough sense to know not to travel out west in the winter. It was a hard journey for a lot of them. But now that spring is here, they are comin' in droves. Won't be no time at all before we see Indian trouble. These people are takin' the Indians' land away from them. The Indian tribes are not gonna stand for it much longer, treaty or no treaty."

This news did not please Jason. Life was changing in many ways, but this change was not a good one. Before all the settlers started coming, the different tribes across the land had felt there was plenty to share—plenty of game and land for everyone. But the white man's invasion of the Indians' territory was reaching a fever pitch. The peace would not hold much longer. Jason thought he had heard enough.

"Well, Colonel," he said, "your news does not make me happy. Think I'll get on over to the tradin' post and sell my stockpile. It's a big one this time. It was a good season." Jason smiled.

"You ain't ridin' back out tonight, are you, son?"

"No, sir, Colonel. I'll be leavin' come first light tomorrow morning."

"Good," said the colonel. "Come back around when you're finished with your business, and we'll go have dinner at Miss Ellie's place."

Jason said, "Sure thing, Colonel. Only this time, I'm buyin'!"

The colonel laughed and said, "I reckon I'll go along with that, son."

Jason left the colonel's office and went directly to the trading post. The folks there had been waiting for him. They knew Jason was due in any day. They were darn near out of furs with all the people coming to the fort to buy their supplies. And the stores back east had already sent a telegram asking for more fox and mink.

"Howdy, Jason," said Lucas, the store owner. "We been expectin' you. I thought that was your rig outside the colonel's office. I'm dang near out of furs in stock with all these new people comin' west."

Jason said, "Then you're in luck today, Lucas. I brought you a bunch of fine-lookin' furs. But I'm tellin' ya, I'm askin' top dollar for all of them." Jason knew Luke was desperate to fill his shelves, so he thought he would up the price of his furs this time. Besides, they were worth it.

"No matter to me," Lucas said. "These people will

pay any price I ask. I'll get my money back and then some when I sell them. Come on, I'll help you carry them in."

Jason and Lucas brought in all of the furs Jason had piled in the buckboard.

After eying them, Lucas said, "Yep! These are some right fine-looking furs, Jason. Name your price."

Jason left Lucas's store with a pocket full of money. He thought, *It wasn't that long ago that I would leave Lucas's place and head right on over to Ike's Saloon. I'd get drunk, get into a fight, and wind up as a guest in one of the colonel's cells. But not this time. Think I'll head over to the general store now.*

Jason had made a list of things to get before he left the cabin—enough supplies to last all spring and summer before his next trip back to the fort in the fall. Inside the general store, he handed his list to the man behind the counter, like he always did. While his supplies were being gathered, Jason walked around the store to see what new things were for sale. He didn't know if they were new items or if he just had never noticed them. Hadn't been any need to look around before.

Jason noticed some bulk material that he thought Tikah would like for the windows of the cabin. It was a light color with small designs on it. Not too fancy and not too manly! *Tikah has been talking about wanting to put a softer touch on the place. Curtains and a tablecloth would be a good start*, he thought. Then he saw a pretty vase and thought, *She might like this for her flowers instead of that ole jar she's been usin'.*

Next he wandered over to some books. *Hmm*, he thought, *learnin' books might be a good idea. Clayton taught Tikah how to speak English words, and with these books, I can*

teach her how to read them, and someday she can teach our son.
Jason decided to buy them.

Finally, Jason's eyes were drawn to a glass display case containing many boxes of beautiful beads. Jason had never seen so many pretty colors and types of beads. He remembered the colorful beads he had seen on Tikah's dress the first time he met her. Jason thought, *Now these would look mighty pretty sewn on Tikah's new dress.* So Jason selected two boxes of them.

"Order's ready, mister," the clerk called from behind the counter.

"Okay," Jason said. "I have a few more things I want to add."

"Sure thing, mister."

Jason carried the bulk material, vase, beads, and learning books over to the counter and set them down.

The clerk looked over the items and said, "You picked some mighty fine things for the missus. Will she be needing some needles and thread for them beads and material?"

Jason said, "Yes! Didn't think of that. Put in what you think she'll need."

The store clerk started adding up Jason's bill. He asked, "Will that be everything?"

"That's it for this trip. My son is just a baby now. Won't be needin' much for him just yet."

The clerk totaled all the things from the list and the things that Jason had added. He gave Jason the bill and said, "You spent a bunch of money here, fella. Sure do appreciate it. Here, I'm going to throw in this here rattle for that little one, free of charge!"

Jason smiled and paid the clerk. He carried the boxes outside and loaded them in the buckboard out front. He covered his supplies with a tarp and tied it down. Then he headed over to the stable to board his horse and store his buckboard for the night. As he neared the stable, Jason noticed a horse for sale. He eyed the animal carefully. The horse was young, strong, and healthy.

A voice behind him asked, "You lookin' to buy a horse, mister?"

Jason turned and saw a man standing out of the sun near the stable. "I might be," he said. "What are ya askin' for it?"

They haggled over a price for a while, and Jason finally agreed. The price was a little high, but with the saddle thrown in, it was worth it. Jason thought it would make a fine horse for Tikah. He took the horse, tied it to the buckboard, and walked both horses and the buckboard into the stable. There he was greeted by the blacksmith, Jake.

"Well, Jason McIvers! You're lookin' right smart these days! Are ya puttin' them up for the night?"

Jason said, "Yes, and can I put the buckboard inside too?"

Jake said, "That will be fifty cents each for the horses and fifty cents for the buckboard, in advance."

Jason paid Jake and walked over to the colonel's office. It had been a long day, and he was hungry. He thought of Miss Ellie's biscuits, and his mouth started to water.

CHAPTER 15

Jason opened the door to Colonel Ashby's outer office and found the colonel standing there.

"Ah, Jason! You ready to eat?"

Jason replied, "Sure am, Colonel. Been thinkin' about Miss Ellie's biscuits all day!"

The two men walked out of the office, and the colonel closed the door behind them.

Down at Miss Ellie's, Jason and the colonel enjoyed a nice supper, complete with fresh-baked apple pie.

"Yep," Jason said at the end of their meal, "best biscuits I ever ate! It's been good to see you again, Colonel, but I reckon it's time for me to get some shut-eye. I'm plannin' an early start in the morning."

"Yep, I reckon so," said the colonel. "You can stay at the bunkhouse again if it suits you, son."

Jason replied, "Thanks, Colonel. That'll be just fine."

The two said their goodbyes and started to go their separate ways, but first the colonel gave Jason a hearty hug and said, "I'm mighty proud of you, son. Safe journey home tomorrow."

Jason said, "Thanks, Colonel. That means a lot!"

Jason fell asleep in his bunk with thoughts of Tikah and Clayton. Soon he would be home with them. He knew Tikah would be pleased to see all that his furs had bought for them.

It was early morning, and the sun was just coming up over the ridge when Jason walked to the stables to pick up his horses and the buckboard. He hitched his horse, tied Tikah's horse to the side of the buckboard, and then started for the gate.

From up in the guard tower, the familiar voice yelled, "Open the gate!"

Jason rode through, and as always, the gate closed quickly behind him.

He wasn't far down the trail when he came upon a young family and a covered wagon stranded on the side of the trail. Jason stopped and asked, "You need a hand?"

The man answered, "Sure could use some help with this wheel, mister. Just about got it fixed but could use some help gettin' it back on."

So Jason steered the buckboard over to the side of the trail. He jumped down and walked over to the wagon. Between the two men, they got the wagon wheel back on and ready to travel in no time at all.

The man said to Jason, "Much obliged, mister."

As Jason turned and started back toward the buckboard, he heard a young voice say, "Hey, mister, want a puppy?"

Jason turned and saw a young boy and girl playing

with three gray puppies. "Well, I don't know," he said. "You givin' 'em away?"

Their father said, "Take one, mister. We came up on them quite a ways back. They were all by themselves along the side of the trail. Weren't no sign of their mother anywhere. We didn't have the heart to leave them there all alone in the heat with no food or water."

Jason walked back toward the children, who were still playing with the puppies. Jason quickly took a liking to the little runt. "What kind of puppies are they?" he asked.

The father answered, "Can't say for sure, but by the looks of 'em, I'd say they might be part wolf."

Jason thought about it for a minute and then decided to take the runt. He picked him up and walked back to the buckboard.

The covered wagon moved on in the direction of the fort. The father hollered back to Jason, "Thanks again, mister!"

Jason decided to let the puppy play a little, hoping it would tire itself out before the long ride home. He thought about how the dog would make a good companion for Clayton and also would be another set of eyes and ears around the place in case something or someone got a little too close to the cabin. Jason watched the puppy sniff all around, as if scouting for something, and the name came to him.

"Scout! That's a right fine name for the little rascal— Scout." Jason called to the puppy and said, "Come on, Scout! Get on back over here."

Scout responded immediately and romped back over

to Jason. Jason smiled as he picked up the puppy and put him on the seat of the buckboard next to him. He slapped the reins against his horse's back, and they were off for the long ride back to the cabin.

It was late afternoon when Jason spotted the cabin off in the distance. He always enjoyed seeing the smoke coming out of the chimney. *Sure makes the place look mighty homey*, he thought as he rode up to the cabin.

When he got a little closer, he could see Tikah standing at the doorway with Clayton in her arms. She had a big smile on her face. "Jason!" she shouted as she waved.

He pulled up to the front yard, jumped off the buckboard, and ran to Tikah. He gave her a big hug, with Clayton pressed between the two of them. He kissed Clayton on the top of his head and said, "You two are sure a sight for sore eyes. I sure missed the both of you!"

Tikah smiled and said, "And we missed you too, Jason, very much. It makes us happy that you are home."

Tikah noticed the little puppy anxiously waiting to get down off the buckboard seat. His little tail wagged as he whimpered to get down. Tikah asked, "Who is your new friend?"

Jason said, "This is Scout. He will be a good companion for Clayton, and he will be a good set of eyes and ears around the place, especially when I'm gone."

Jason walked over to the buckboard and lifted Scout down to the ground. Once again, the pup immediately started sniffing around, looking under and behind strange new things.

Jason asked, "Do you like him?

Tikah said, "Yes, I do, and so will Clayton when he gets a little older."

Then Jason untied Tikah's horse and walked it over to the porch. He said, "This horse and saddle are for you. Best that we each have our own horse now."

Tikah was speechless as she looked at her new horse in utter disbelief. Finally, she said, "Jason, you are a wonderful husband. Clayton and I are so happy to be here with you." Tikah couldn't hide her curiosity as she looked around Jason to study the tarp covering the buckboard.

Jason said, "I brought back quite a haul from the fort. I better get it unloaded before it gets dark."

"I will take Clayton inside, and you can show us what you got. Come, Scout," she said.

Tikah and Jason were both surprised that Scout followed Tikah into the cabin when she called him. Tikah sat on her chair by the hearth with Clayton on her lap, and Scout sat next to her.

Jason tied up Tikah's horse and then began to carry in armload after armload of supplies. Initially, what Tikah saw did not impress her much: bags of flour, sugar, and coffee and the other usual supplies. Jason was toying with Tikah. He knew she was probably hoping for something for Clayton, so he saved the things she would admire the most for last.

Tikah's eyes lit up when Jason came into the room with the bulk material. He said, "I thought you could use this to put your 'soft touch' on this man's cabin."

Tikah's smile was still on her face when Jason brought in the two boxes of beads. They were a quite a surprise, and Tikah said, "Oh, Jason, they are beautiful. They will do much to decorate my dresses with color and beauty."

"Hold on," Jason said. "I'm not done yet!"

He went back outside for one more load. He brought in the needles and thread, the vase for Tikah's flowers, the learning books, and Clayton's rattle. He placed everything on the table and said, "That's all of it!"

Tikah handed Clayton to Jason. He held the baby while Tikah picked up each item. She admired them all and said, "All these wonderful things, Jason. What did you buy for yourself?"

Jason said, "Nothing I need. I already got everything I could want right here with you and Clayton."

Tikah smiled and asked, "Did you spend all your fur money?"

"No," Jason said. "We have money left to buy our winter supplies when the time comes. The furs brought a large sum of money this season, more than ever before. I got top dollar for each of them. Lucas bought every fur I had."

Tikah said, "You are a good trapper, Jason. You do good work to prepare your furs for selling. Someday you will teach Clayton to trap as you do."

"Yes, and someday soon, I will teach you how to read by using these learning books, and then you will teach Clayton."

Tikah picked up the learning books. She looked at the colorful pictures and said, "Yes, Jason. I want to learn to read the words I speak, and someday I will teach Clayton. But now we will have supper, and you can tell me all the goings-on at the fort."

Jason put Clayton in his cradle and rocked him a little before he said, "All right. But first I'm going to put the horses and buckboard away."

Tikah set the table for supper and put some spring flowers she had picked earlier that day in her new vase. She stood back to admire how pretty they looked.

When Jason came back inside, he washed his hands and face before he sat at the table. He would tell Tikah all the news from the fort and about his visit with the colonel and the fine dinner they'd had at Miss Ellie's place. But he had decided not to tell her what the colonel had said about some folks not being too keen on the idea of him marrying Tikah.

Tikah had prepared a nice meal for their supper. Jason was amazed at how she could make food taste so good. After dinner Tikah cleared the table and washed the dishes while Jason sat on his chair by the hearth, holding Clayton. Scout sat on the floor next to them. When Tikah finished her chores, she sat on her chair next to Jason.

Jason said, "I think tomorrow I'll ride out and collect all my traps and put them away till winter. It will take the better part of the day, but I should be back by late afternoon. Then we need to get our garden planted. The weather is right for it. And then I think I'll get to work on makin' those rockin' chairs!"

Tikah smiled and said, "So much to do, Jason. But we need to add one more chore to your list—we must start with the learning books. We could sit together at the end of each day, after our chores are done and Clayton has gone to sleep. I am anxious to learn so I can teach Clayton someday."

"Yes!" Jason said. "The learning books! We'll start right away!" Jason was happy that he had bought the books. *It's hard gettin' by if a person can't read or write,* he thought, although most people he knew could not. The smartest person he knew was the colonel.

It was finally time to end the day. There was much work to do in the morning. Tikah thought, *When Jason leaves to gather his traps, I will ride out with Clayton to see my mother. She does not know what became of me, and she does not know that I have a son. I am very proud of my life, and I want to share my happiness with her, but I think I will stay silent about this to Jason. I am not sure he would want me to ride that distance and back alone, but it is not as far away as he thinks.*

Jason and Tikah got into bed together. Jason leaned over and blew out the lantern. They missed sleeping together the night before and were glad to be back in each other's arms again.

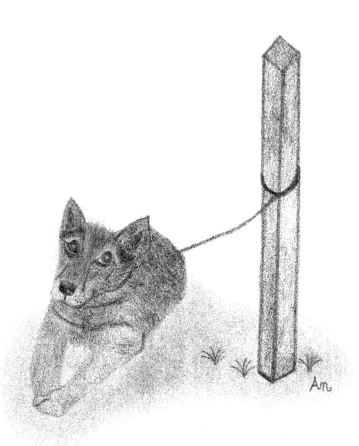

CHAPTER 16

Morning came fast this day. Jason would have liked to sleep longer, but Clayton, Scout, and daylight were telling him it was time to get up.

Tikah was already up and had breakfast waiting for Jason. She was excited about riding out when he left. Tikah fed Clayton while Jason ate his breakfast. Soon after Jason was ready to leave. He hugged Tikah and kissed Clayton on the top of the head and said as he went out the door, "I will be back by late afternoon." He looked over at Scout and said, "Take good care of my family while I'm gone."

Jason and Tikah both laughed as Scout romped around and played with a toy that Tikah had made for him. Tikah said, "Someday he will make a fine watchdog!"

Jason closed the door. He walked to the shed and saddled up his horse and then rode off. Tikah quickly wrapped Clayton in a swaddling cloth and tied up Scout on the front porch. He was too young to roam free yet. She put out a bowl of food and a bowl of water for him and then saddled up her horse and rode out. It was only a two-hour ride to where her people lived.

When Tikah arrived, she rode right to her mother's lodge. The women around the lodges seemed happy to see Tikah and were very curious about the baby in the swaddling cloth.

Tikah got off her horse and walked toward the lodge, calling out to her mother as she entered. Her mother was sitting on the dirt floor of her lodge that was covered with a woven blanket. Tikah's mother sat with her back to the entrance while working on her loom. When she heard her daughter's voice, she called out Tikah's name. She got up and turned to greet Tikah, and when she did, her eyes went right to Clayton in his swaddling cloth. She didn't know what to make of this, and at first she said nothing.

Tikah stood there with a smile on her face and extended her arms, as if to hand Clayton to her mother. She said, "This is your grandson, Clayton."

Tikah's mother stopped after one step toward Tikah. She did not reach for Clayton, but she did look at him with inquisitive eyes. She stared at Clayton, examining his facial features. She likely also noticed that the baby had light skin despite his dark black hair.

Tikah could see that her mother did not wish to hold the baby, and she did not ask Tikah to sit down. So Tikah held Clayton close to her chest and began her story about Jason, Pale One, and how she had become Jason's wife. Tikah's mother still did not speak.

"Well, what do you think of your grandson?" Tikah asked.

Tikah's mother said, "You shame me, and your baby shames me and our people."

Tikah's smile quickly turned to a frown. She felt the blood drain from her face as her mother continued.

"You know it is against the Opoka way for any of our people to marry outside our nation. It was forbidden even for Pale One. He asked your father many times for permission to marry you, and each time your father told him no, it could not be so. Your baby will be an outcast; he will not belong to the Opoka people, and he will not belong in the white man's world. You shame your people even more by naming your son with Pale One's white man's name, not even the name your father gave Pale One. Your visit does not please me, and I wish for you to leave now."

Tikah could hardly believe her mother's words. She thought, *How can my mother be so cruel? Yes, it is forbidden to marry someone not of our kind, but that she could be so cruel to Clayton really saddens me.* Tikah had never thought of her marriage to Jason as shameful. Jason was everything her mother would want in a man who married her daughter. Jason's pale skin made no difference to Tikah. The child they shared had come into this world from love, powerful love between a man and a woman. How could this be so bad? Tikah's thoughts were interrupted by the sound of her mother's voice.

"Leave now, Tikah, and do not return again."

Tikah turned, and without saying another word, she walked out of her mother's lodge. She got back on her horse and slowly rode off. She did not make eye contact with the others, and she did not have a smile on her face like she had when she rode in. She heard soft whispers coming from the women, and she could only guess that they were confused about what had just happened.

It was a sad ride home for Tikah. She thought of her great love for Jason and their son. She had not expected the harsh words of her mother. Tikah decided right then that she no longer wanted to be a part of the Opoka Nation. From that day forward, she would be content to live only in the white man's world. *This is where I belong now*, she thought. *I will not speak of this to Jason. He must not know.*

Tikah arrived back at the cabin before Jason. She untied Scout, and he ran in front of her into the cabin. Tikah had plenty of time to put her horse away, quickly pick some wildflowers, and start supper. She fed Clayton and then put him in his cradle. He quickly fell asleep from the motion of the rocking. Scout played quietly with his toy next to the cradle. Joy came back into Tikah's heart. She felt content being back in her home. Somehow, she would have to put the life she had once known as an Opoka Indian behind her. She was now an outcast but found comfort in knowing that she and Clayton would live a wonderful life in the white man's world.

Scout's ears perked up. He quit playing with his toy and ran to the door. Tikah saw this and did not know what think of it. Just then, the door opened, and Jason walked in.

"Jason," she said, "I did not hear you on the porch. If not for Scout, I would not have known you were home."

Jason said, "I knew Scout would be my eyes and

ears whenever I was away, but I wanted to test him just the same. I am happy he is attentive and that his senses alerted you."

Clayton stirred in his cradle at the sound of Jason's voice. Jason walked over to the baby and picked him up. He raised him high over his head and smiled.

Tikah said, "Come, sit down, and we will have supper."

Jason noticed that Tikah had used some of the material he brought home for a tablecloth and had put fresh flowers in the vase. Jason was happy to be home. After supper he played with Clayton and then put him back in his cradle when it was time to go to sleep. Scout settled down next to Clayton's cradle as Tikah and Jason got into bed. Jason leaned over and blew out the lantern.

They both lay there quietly, thinking about what they each had learned recently but dared not speak of to the other. Jason's conversation with the colonel the day before played over in his mind. Tikah thought about her mother's cruel words earlier that day. As they lay beside each other, they both realized that not everyone would be happy about their life together, but that did not matter to either one of them. The prejudiced feelings of others were something they would probably always have to live with. Jason rolled over and held Tikah. They did not allow such thoughts to come between them.

The following morning, Jason and Tikah decided it would be a good day to plant their garden. Tikah went to the dresser drawer and took out the packages of seeds that Jason had brought home from the fort. Jason carried Clayton's cradle out onto the porch, and Tikah put Clayton in it. She pushed it a little to start the rocking motion. Scout sat down next to the cradle and watched everything all around him.

It was a good day; they prepared the soil, dug the trenches, and then planted carrots, squash, kale, corn, onions, beets, and radishes. Tikah had saved some old potatoes that had begun to grow roots from the eyes, so they planted them too. The well was not far from the garden, so it would not be hard to get pails of water to the plants.

The summer wore on. Jason tended to chores outside and mended parts of the corral that needed tending to. The shed was in desperate need of repair, so he worked on that also. His traps were all sorted and oiled. He had them hanging on the wall in the shed, ready for the winter season.

Tikah enjoyed covering the windows with some of the material she had from the fort. She was proud of how the cabin looked and how the garden was growing. But she was most proud of how beautiful her dress looked with the many beautiful beads she had sewn on it. This would be a dress for special wear. She had made herself another dress shortly after Clayton was born, so that was the dress she usually wore now.

Tikah made a little pair of moccasins for Clayton. He was not walking yet but they will keep his feet warm in the coming fall and winter months., She also made him a little pair of buckskin britches to protect his legs and knees when he crawled around.

Tikah was making good progress with the learning books. Jason was amazed at how smart she was and how eager she was to learn to read.

The months turned to years. Soon Clayton and Scout were two years old, and Clayton had long since outgrown his moccasins and buckskin britches. Tikah was back to wearing her dress made for a growing belly. She was with child again, and they were looking forward to welcoming a new baby brother or sister for Clayton. Tikah had not ventured far from the cabin. She was content with her life and felt no reason to leave. Jason still went to the fort twice a year, once in the spring to sell his furs and buy the spring and summer supplies and once in the fall for their winter supplies. Another two trapping seasons had come and gone. The price of fur had gone up, and so had the demand for them. It was another profitable season for Jason.

Sadly on Jason's recent trip to the fort he learned that the colonel had passed away. Jason asked around but no one really knew what happened. They said he was fine one day and gone the next. So Jason went to see the colonel's private medic to ask what happened and the medic told Jason he suspected the colonel died of a heart attack. The colonel had a proper military funeral and Jason was glad he was there to attend the ceremony and burial.

There had been a lot of changes, some good and some bad. The Indian uprisings had not stayed just between the different tribes. The tribes eventually had put their differences aside to focus on their one common enemy: the white man. The white settlers had been coming in more numbers than anyone had ever expected. They took from the Indians the land that they had lived on for many generations. They hunted the game almost to extinction. The many tribes became angry; they agreed on treaty after treaty, but the white man broke them all.

The Indian tribes had no other choice but to migrate north into Canada, to avoid being captured by the army and put in confinement on reservations. The government had promised to take care of the Indians if they surrendered and turned in their weapons, but the government did not keep that promise either. The conditions on the reservations were appalling. Once-proud Indian nations were reduced to begging for meager handouts.

Jason learned about these developments when he went to the fort. He would come home and tell Tikah the sad news. Even though Tikah had not had any contact with the Opokas for a long time now, she was saddened to learn of their plight and wondered what ever had become of her mother.

Tikah and Jason had a hard time understanding why the nations could not live in harmony, but it was no longer meant to be. Settlements were showing up everywhere, and the army's occupation of the once-peaceful Indian land was inexcusable. But Jason and Tikah remained impartial and lived their lives isolated, as they always had.

Clayton's baby brother was also born in the spring, and this time it was Jason who wanted Tikah's approval of a name for their new son. One evening after supper, they sat in their chairs by the hearth, and Jason said, "Tikah, I have thought of a name for our son, and I hope that you will agree. I would like to name him Tyson, after Colonel Ashby. The colonel was like a father to me right up to the day he died. If it were not for the colonel, who knows what would have become of me? He took me under his wing back when I was an unruly drunk. He always stuck by me no matter what, and most of all, he was downright happy when I told him about you."

He took a deep breath and continued on, "I never told you, Tikah, but not everybody was agreeable to us getting married. Most folks couldn't understand what a white man saw in an Indian girl. It was not acceptable. But I never let that kind of talk get in the way of my love for you. The colonel, he warned me about them folks' feelins, but he did not feel that way. He was happy for me, and he was mighty proud of the man I became after you came into my life. It ain't the same when I ride into the fort now, with him bein' gone. Well, anyways, that is why I would like to name our son Tyson."

Clayton and Scout were playing in the cabin, totally oblivious to what was going on around them, while the baby lay sleeping in the same cradle that Clayton had once slept in.

Tikah looked over at them and smiled. "I think Tyson would be a fine name for our son," she said. "I would like to honor your wish and call our son Tyson." After a short pause she said, "There is something I wish to tell you, Jason, that I have kept silent about for two years. Two years ago, on the day when you rode out to collect your traps at the end of the season, I took Clayton and rode to visit my mother."

"I did not know your people lived so close!" Jason said.

Tikah said, "It is about a two-hour ride east of here. You do not trap in that area, so you would not know how close they were. It was not a happy visit, Jason. My mother was not happy that I had married a white man. It is forbidden by my people; even Pale One was not given permission to marry me. But even worse, my mother said some very hurtful things about Clayton."

Tears rolled down her cheeks as she continued. "She said our baby did not belong in either world. She said because he is half-white, he does not belong in the Opoka Nation, and he does not belong in the white man's world. She would not even hold her grandson. She told me to leave and never return."

Jason was stunned to hear Tikah's words. Tikah was a strong woman, and he had never seen her cry before. He knew how badly Tikah's mother had hurt her. He got up, walked over to her, and wiped the tears from her eyes. Tikah stood up, and they hugged each other as Scout kept a watchful eye on both of them.

They sat back down, and Jason said, "Tikah, I am sorry you felt such pain and kept it within you. We have both learned that there will be people in both nations who do not approve of our love and our life together. But that should be of no concern to us. I did not tell you about what the colonel told me for, I guess, the same reason you did not tell me about your mother; we did not want to worry each other over what others may think of us. What others think of us can be hurtful. But there are others who do not see the color of our skin, only the goodness that is in our hearts. Those are the people we will surround ourselves with."

Tikah noticed the quietness around the cabin. She looked over at Scout and Clayton and saw that they both had fallen asleep on the floor where they had been playing. Jason and Tikah laughed.

"Well," Jason said, "guess it's time for all of us to get some shut-eye. Tomorrow is a new day."

Tikah put Clayton to bed while Jason stoked the fire. Tikah and Jason got undressed and got into bed. Jason put his arms around Tikah as she snuggled close to him.

CHAPTER **17**

The years passed quickly. Clayton and Tyson grew to be handsome young men and fine trappers, just like their father, and soon the boys had homesteads of their own.

Clayton married an Opoka girl. She and her parents had been migrating north, trying to keep hidden from the soldiers who were rounding up the Indians and forcing them to live on reservations. One day while out trapping with his sons, Jason had come upon them. They were frightened, hungry, and cold. Jason was able to convince them that he meant no harm. Jason, Clayton, and Tyson encouraged the family to accompany them to their cabin to get warm and eat some hot food. Jason spoke of his Opoka wife and how she would welcome them into their home.

The young daughter was about the same age as Clayton. Her name was Wachikah, and she and Clayton immediately took a liking to each other. When it came time for Wachikah's parents to continue their journey,

Wachikah wanted to stay behind. Her parents had become very fond of Tikah and her family. They had known of Tikah previously but had never heard what had become of her after she rode out from their village many years ago. Wachikah's parents knew it would be safe for Wachikah to stay and live with Tikah's family, rather than risk the unknown of traveling north to escape from the soldiers. They felt they had lived the best years of their lives, but Wachikah still had her whole life ahead of her. It was a sad parting, but it was for the best. Wachikah never saw her parents again. Wachikah and Tikah became very close.

Tyson married a girl he met at the fort. Her name was Elizabeth, and she had come out west with her parents. Tragically, one day while they were still traveling, their wagon had hit a large hole in the ground and overturned. Both of her parents had been killed instantly under the heavy weight of the wagon. Elizabeth had been able to jump off the wagon before it rolled.

Grief-stricken, Elizabeth had continued on with the others in the wagon train until they reached the fort. She then had chosen to stay at the fort while trying to decide what she wanted to do with her life: stay out west or go back where she had come from. When Miss Ellie heard about the tragedy, she offered Elizabeth a job helping out at her place and waiting tables. Miss Ellie took Elizabeth under her wing and provided her with the spare room upstairs to stay in as payment for her work. The two became very fond of each other. Miss Ellie was not married and did not have children of her own. Yet she had a very kind heart and grew to love Elizabeth as if she were her own daughter.

Tyson met Elizabeth when Jason took Clayton and Tyson to Miss Ellie's for supper, to celebrate after selling their furs one spring. The boys had grown up hearing their father's stories about always treating himself to a fine meal at Miss Ellie's after a successful fur season and about how he had always eaten there with Colonel Ashby. It had become a tradition for Jason, Clayton, and Tyson to go to Miss Ellie's for a special meal at the end of every trapping season.

One day late in the spring, Miss Ellie took sick and never recovered. Elizabeth was with her on that sad day. Miss Ellie told Elizabeth, "I am an old woman now and I have lived a good life." Miss Ellie also told Elizabeth that having Elizabeth in her life was the best thing that ever happened to her. Miss Ellie's last words to Elizabeth were, "I love you. You have been like a daughter to me."

When Miss Ellie died, Elizabeth was heartbroken. No one around the fort was qualified to take over the restaurant, and it closed. It was then that Tyson convinced Elizabeth to come live with his family. Elizabeth was someone who looked into a person's heart and soul, far beyond what was on the outside. So it did not matter to her that some members of Tyson's family were Indian or that Tyson was half-Indian.

For the weddings of both her sons, Tikah wore a special buckskin dress that was beautifully adorned with the beads Jason had given her many years ago. When grandchildren came along, Clayton's children, Matthew

FRANCES BORICCHIO

and Sarah, slept in the same cradle Clayton and his brother had slept in when they were babies. Jason made another cradle for Tyson's children, James and Rebecca. All the children were taught to read and write using the same learning books that Jason had used to teach Tikah and that Tikah had used to teach Clayton and Tyson. Clayton and Tyson's families established homes near each other, and there was a close bond between the brothers' families and Jason and Tikah.

Clayton and Tyson wanted their parents to be closer to their homesteads, so the brothers built a new cabin for their mother and father to replace the old place that the boys had grown up in. They even built a proper barn for Jason. Jason and Tikah were happy to be near their sons and daughters-in-law. Tikah and Jason loved doting on their grandchildren, and Tikah had a very special bond with Wachikah and Elizabeth.

One cold winter night, Jason and Tikah sat by the hearth in their rocking chairs, which Jason had finally found time to make after the boys took over the trapping lines. They reminisced about their life together and all that they had been through, including some bad times but mostly good ones. Tikah reminded Jason about Scout and what a good dog he had turned out to be. He had been a good playmate for Clayton and Tyson and had grown to be a very good watchdog too. Scout had lived a long life, and the day he passed on had been sad for everyone.

They had never gotten another dog after Scout, who had been one of a kind, with his keen ears and sharp eyes. Jason had always thought those characteristics were due to Scout being part wolf. Scout was not aggressive by nature, especially around the boys, but Jason was sure he was capable of defending his family if someone ever threatened the boys or Tikah.

It had been a long time since Tikah had spoken of the Opoka people, but she thought of them often and felt the need to speak of them with Jason on this night. Even though her last visit with her mother many years ago had not gone well, Tikah still had compassion for her mother. She hoped that her mother and her people had made it to Canada to escape from the soldiers and had been able to live out the rest of their lives in peace. She would never know.

Life had continued to change over the years. The gold rush had dried up in 1855, and many settlers had left, but many more had come to work in the few gold, silver, and copper mines that remained. The Civil War had broken out in 1861 and killed thousands, oftentimes with brother fighting against brother and father against son. Clayton and Tyson shuddered at the thought. Like their parents, they too could never understand why people would not accept each other's differences and live in harmony.

It had been a long time since Jason had made the trip to the fort; it was a difficult ride for him now. The once desolate prairie between their place and the fort was all built-up, with homesteads everywhere along the way. Jason would hardly recognize the fort anymore either. It had changed a lot, with new stores and shops opening and old ones closing. With the Indian threat gone, stores and establishments were springing up all around, outside the confines of the fort.

Clayton and Tyson now went to the fort twice a year, just as Jason once had, once to sell their furs in the spring and once in the fall to buy the winter supplies for all three families. When they got back after every trip, they always had a large family supper together, and the boys told the family the news they had learned at the fort. It was hard for all of them to hear what was happening around them. Jason wasn't even sure if the boys told them everything. *I reckon it's better that way,* Jason often thought.

The McIvers' furs were still the best-selling furs at the fort, and they remained the top quality they had always been. Orders for their furs continued to come over the telegraph for shipments back east. The boys were still able to name their price; there was no real competition.

Jason and Tikah had lived a long and happy life together. Now in their elder years, living in their comfortable log home near their family, they were content to sit together by the hearth on their rocking chairs and enjoy the warmth of the fire. The flames mesmerized them, as they always had. The wood crackled and popped, and they watched the embers on the hearth slowly burn out.

Jason reached for Tikah's hand, and she put her hand in his. Jason said, "I think it's time to get some shut-eye."

Printed in the United States
By Bookmasters